SCIENCE FAIR BOOK

By Samantha Margles

SCHOLASTIC INC.

Photo credits:
Chalkboard image © Maridav/Shutterstock, Inc.
Math diagrams © Inga Nielsen/Shutterstock, Inc.

ISBN 978-0-545-52099-7

12 11 10 9 8 7 6 5 4 3 2 1   13 14 15 16 17 18/0

Art direction: **Rick DeMonico**
Interior design: **Rocco Melillo**
Cover design: **Cheung Tai**
Diagrams: **Michael Massen**

Printed in the U.S.A.   40
First printing, September 2013

CONTENTS:

INTRODUCTION

Rebel leaders and the Jedi are put to the test as they face off against the evil Empire. Whether it's Queen Amidala and Qui-Gon Jinn, or Luke Skywalker and Princess Leia, the heroes of the epic saga are made up of determined and passionate people who are also masters of incredible scientific knowledge. They travel between star systems to visit different planets, tap into the powers of the Force, and utilize advanced technology to survive uninhabitable climates and dangerous situations.

Have you ever wondered how much of the science-fiction world of *Star Wars* is based on real-life science? Are some of the situations in the films possible or simply part of a fantastic story? Now you have a chance to find out.

In this book we've pulled together an assortment of experiments and activities that examine the science of *Star Wars*. Some of the experiments are inspired by the planets, creatures, droids, and technology from the films, and some go a step further to answer related scientific questions you'll find exciting and fun. Perhaps one day you'll find yourself on a path toward becoming a scientist and explorer of galaxies far, far away! May the Force be with you!

THE FORCE AND SCIENCE: THE SCIENTIFIC METHOD

A Jedi knows it's important to be mindful when undertaking tasks — scientists work the same way. The scientific method allows scientists to address their investigations with precision and accuracy. Here's how to use this book as a Jedi scientist:

1) Understand Your Mission: The opening paragraph for each of the experiments in this book will present a scenario or question to investigate. Read this before you start and identify what you're attempting to learn.

2) Know Your Tools: For each experiment we provide a detailed list of the materials you'll need and provide an idea of how much the materials may cost to acquire. We also give you an estimate of the length of time you'll need to run the experiment. Make sure you have all the materials you need before you begin any investigation.

3) Know the Way: Each experiment has detailed steps for how to perform the necessary test. Before you begin, read all the way through all the steps to be sure you know what's expected of you.

4) Use the Force to See the Future: Before scientists start to work, they make what's called a hypothesis. This is their best guess for the outcome of an experiment based on everything they know about what's involved. Before you begin, focus on the information you already have and try to predict the outcome of your experiment. You can write this in a notebook and see if you were right.

5) Find Results: Now you should be ready to run your experiment. Carefully follow the steps provided and log all the necessary information in your notebook as you go. When you finish, compare your results with your hypothesis. Was the Force strong with you? Did you see in advance what the results would be?

The Secret: Sometimes you'll find "THE SECRET" at the end of an experiment. This section offers further information on the process or results of your experiment. If you don't want to know in advance what may happen, we recommend you skip reading this until you've finished your work.

DIFFICULTY LEVELS:

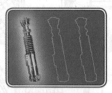

One lightsaber means the experiment is simple. You can probably try this alone and find the materials at home.

Two lightsabers indicate you may need an adult to help you with the experiment and may have to get some materials at a store or order them online.

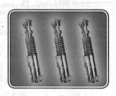

Three lightsabers tell you that an adult should help you with at least some part of the experiment and with purchasing materials.

Cost Calculator: For the most part, you'll be able to find the materials for these experiments at home or at the grocery store. Once in a while they require more technical equipment or items that may cost slightly more. At the start of each experiment you'll see dollar signs.

One dollar sign means the materials you need will cost less than $15.

Two dollar signs mean the materials will cost between $15 and $25.

Three dollar signs mean the total cost will be more than $25.

PART I
IN A GALAXY FAR, FAR AWAY . . . .

MAKE YOUR OWN CLOUDS

Cloud City, the beautiful and productive domain of Lando Calrissian, is a majestic metropolis floating high above the gas planet of Bespin. Unfortunately, when Han Solo and Princess Leia go there to hide from the Empire, they fall into a trap laid by Darth Vader. But Cloud City's stunning landscape has nothing to do with politics or war. It would be hard to build a city on clouds here on our planet, but it is possible to create a situation that demonstrates how clouds form in the first place.

WHAT YOU NEED:

- 5" x 5" square of rubber, or a large rubber glove cut to those dimensions

- Large (approximately 1 quart) glass jar

- Water

- Matches*

- Tongs or pliers

- Heavy-duty rubber bands

- Desk lamp

- Black paper or fabric

TIME REQUIRED: 15 MINUTES

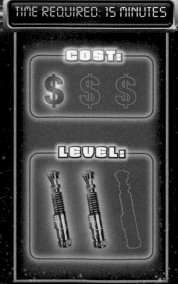

COST:

$ $ $

LEVEL:

* You may need an adult to handle the matches for you.

WHAT TO DO:

Step 1: Gather your materials and have them all within reach. Make sure your glass jar is clean and free of labels. Rinse the inside of the jar and let a small amount of water remain in the bottom of it, just enough to cover the bottom surface. This will be your "cloud chamber."

Step 2: If an adult is handling the matches for you, have your helper light a match and let it burn for a few seconds. Next, use the tongs or pliers to hold the matchstick, blow it out, then quickly move the smoking matchstick inside the jar for a few seconds. The goal is to hold the smoking matchstick inside the jar long enough to release some smoke, then remove it and cover the mouth of the jar without the smoke escaping.

Step 3: Quickly, so the smoke doesn't escape, cover the mouth of the jar with the rubber square and secure it in place using the rubber bands. The rubber should be held firmly enough that you can pull and press on it without it coming loose.

Step 4: Move the jar around so the water on the bottom coats the sides of the jar.

Step 5: While you watch the contents of the jar, push in the rubber square for a few seconds. Next, pinch the rubber square in the middle and pull it slightly out, away from the jar. Pull it at least an inch, more if it seems like your seal will hold. You can hold the black paper or fabric behind the jar to improve the visibility of your results.

THE Secret:

Clouds form when water vapor combines with matter in the air under just the right pressure. First, there must be very small pieces of material, like dust, in the air for the water to cling to. Second, when the pressure in the atmosphere is decreased, vaporized water molecules will change to liquid and stick to the dust. Increased pressure causes the water to evaporate (become vapor) and move back into the air, forming a cloud in the air surrounding the dust. In this experiment, the smoke from the match provides the particles for the water to cling to. Pulling out the rubber decreases the pressure in the jar and allows the water to condense (become more concentrated) on the smoke particles, forming a cloud. An increase in temperature will cause more evaporation and the cloud to diminish. What is likely to happen if you hold your cloud chamber in front of the light for too long?

FORMING MINERAL DEPOSITS

When Qui-Gon Jinn and Obi-Wan Kenobi first visit Naboo to negotiate with the Trade Federation, they are forced to flee for their lives. Jar Jar Binks brings them to his home in the underwater city of Otoh Gunga and helps them secure a ship in which to travel to the capital city of Theed. On their journey, they must constantly dodge beautiful but dangerous mineral formations in the caves. These formations are made up of stalactites (which hang down) and stalagmites (which point upward). Mineral deposits such as these can take hundreds of thousands of years to build up in nature. Luckily, we don't have to wait that long to observe how they form in this fun and easy experiment.

WHAT YOU NEED:

TIME REQUIRED: 15 MINUTES

- 2 large jars
- Hot water
- Epsom salts
- Spoon for stirring
- Cotton or wool string, about 1/8" thick and 18" long
- Something to weigh down the ends of the strings, like fishing lure weights, heavy beads, or paper clips, or even a few dimes
- Cookie baking sheet

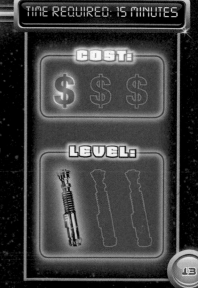

COST:

$ $ $

LEVEL:

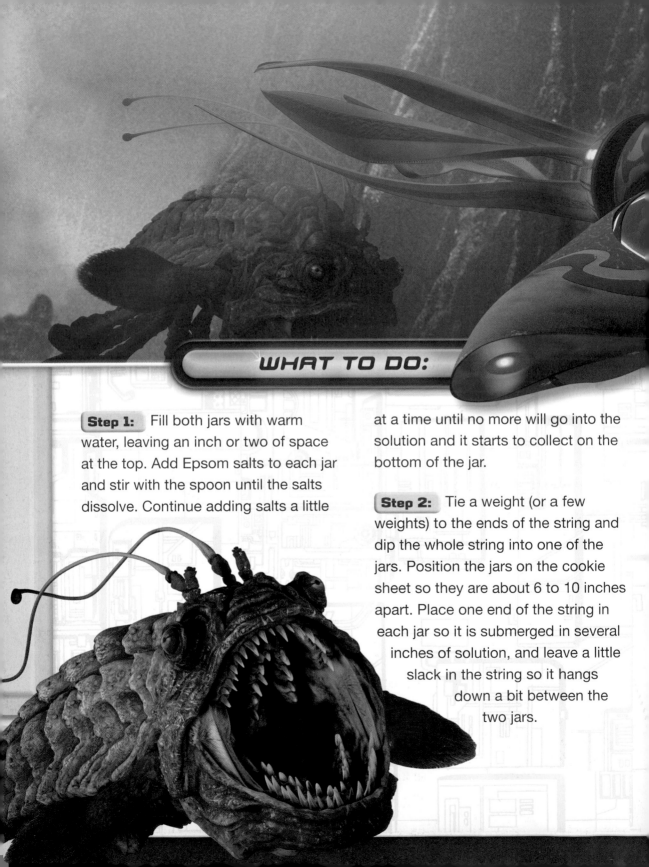

WHAT TO DO:

Step 1: Fill both jars with warm water, leaving an inch or two of space at the top. Add Epsom salts to each jar and stir with the spoon until the salts dissolve. Continue adding salts a little at a time until no more will go into the solution and it starts to collect on the bottom of the jar.

Step 2: Tie a weight (or a few weights) to the ends of the string and dip the whole string into one of the jars. Position the jars on the cookie sheet so they are about 6 to 10 inches apart. Place one end of the string in each jar so it is submerged in several inches of solution, and leave a little slack in the string so it hangs down a bit between the two jars.

Step 3: Leave the jars to sit for several days. Every day or two, observe your setup to see if any changes have occurred. Do you see the accumulation of mineral formations on the string and below the string on the cookie sheet? These are your very own stalactites and stalagmites!

THE Secret:

Stalactites and stalagmites form when minerals dissolved in water (like limestone) come out of a solution (a mixture of two or more substances) and collect at a specific point. When a mineral solution drips slowly from a high point like the roof of a cave (or a dangling string), the mineral has a chance to change into a solid before the water drops, like an icicle. On the ground below, any mineral remaining in the drop of water can form a solid as the water evaporates.

TESTING FOR OXYGEN IN WATER

The underwater site of Otoh Gunga is where the Gungans live, in bubble cities surrounded by vast and dangerous waters. Though the amphibious Gungans can live both on land and in water, the creatures surrounding their home are strictly aquatic. Did you ever wonder what it takes to support life underwater? It takes much of the same stuff we need here on land, including oxygen! In this experiment, you'll test the amount of oxygen available to aquatic creatures under different circumstances, and find out just what impacts the availability of that essential element.

WHAT YOU NEED:

- Dissolved oxygen test kit*

- 3 or 4 small aquariums

- Pond water or tap water

- Clean buckets or empty gallon jugs

- Elodea sprigs**

- Compost or decaying matter from the bottom of a pond, lake, or forest floor

- Notebook and pencil or pen

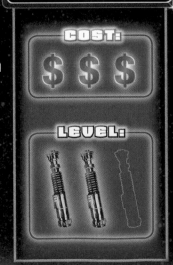

TIME REQUIRED: 1 TO 2 HOURS INITIALLY, A WEEK TO SIT, ANOTHER HOUR FOR FOLLOW-UP TESTS

COST:

$ $ $

LEVEL:

*Dissolved oxygen test kits can be purchased online or through science experiment providers for $30 to $50.

**Elodea is a common freshwater aquatic plant. It can be purchased from pet stores or online suppliers for around $5. Other aquarium plants would also work.

WHAT TO DO:

Step 1: Decide if you're going to use pond water or tap water. Either will work fine, but water from a pond or lake will tell you what oxygen levels are like in a natural ecosystem. Fill your aquariums with tap water, or large buckets or gallon jugs of water that you have collected from your work site.

Step 2: Using your test kit, check your water for the initial level of dissolved oxygen. If you're using pond or lake water, you'll want to test the water at the site and not from the samples you bring home. This will give you the most accurate reading of the naturally occurring dissolved oxygen.

Follow the instructions in your kit. This will involve adding three different packets or tablets of chemicals to your water sample (which should have no air bubbles present in it). These packets will cause a series of color changes in your sample as different substances form and precipitate out of the water. The final step will have you add a chemical— one drop at a time—until the water sample turns clear. The number of drops you add will correspond to the amount of dissolved oxygen in your sample, usually in parts per million (ppm). This unit refers to how many molecules of oxygen are present for every million molecules of your sample. In your notebook, record the quantity of dissolved oxygen found in your initial sample.

Step 3: Create three or four experimental setups using your aquariums. Label them #1 to #4. Fill #1 with only water. Fill #2 with water and several elodea plants. Don't overcrowd the tank, but add enough to spread evenly throughout the space. In #3, lay the compost or dead organic matter on the bottom before adding the water. In #4, you can test the impact of both dead or decaying matter and elodea plants.

These four setups will allow you to test the change in dissolved oxygen in several instances: #1, with no impact from plants or decaying matter; #2, in the presence of plants; #3, in the presence of decaying matter; and #4, in the presence of both plants and decaying matter, which approximates a natural situation. Let these aquariums sit somewhere, preferably with a constant temperature, for a week or more.

Step 4: Using your kit, test the dissolved oxygen content of each of your setups. Record this data in your notebook and compare the results with your data from the first day. What changes took place? Can you think of how to explain your observations? If you can, leave the setups for another week or more, test them again, and make further comparisons.

THE Secret:

Dissolved oxygen enters water in two ways. First, oxygen can simply dissolve from the air into the water. This commonly happens when water is disturbed by waves or rain. Second, aquatic plants produce oxygen just like their terrestrial relatives (those plants that live on land) do. Oxygen is used when decaying organic matter is broken down by organisms such as microscopic bacteria. The use and production of oxygen are essential parts of a healthy, balanced ecosystem. What would happen if there was decaying organic matter and no live plants? Or if the quantity of decaying matter was so great that the plants couldn't keep up? Would animals living underwater be able to survive without adequate oxygen? This gives you some idea of the impact that decaying matter can have on aquatic ecosystems, and the importance of plants, even underwater!

HOW TO MAKE A HYGROMETER

Luke Skywalker grew up on the desert planet Tatooine, on a moisture farm. On the desiccated (thoroughly dried up) planet, moisture farmers harvest water out of the air that can be used for agriculture or for drinking. This technique relies on the fact that even in desert ecosystems, a certain amount of moisture remains in the atmosphere. But how much?

Here's how to construct a hygrometer, a tool that measures atmospheric humidity. It can also determine which days or what time of day might be best for getting your water vaporator up and running.

WHAT YOU NEED:

- Small, thin piece of wood or Styrofoam, approximately 5" x 10"

- Flat piece of thin plastic that will hold its shape, like the cover of a report binder

- 2 small nails or thumbtacks

- 3 long strands of hair, approximately 8"

- 1 dime

- Glue

- Clear tape

- Hammer

- Scissors

- Rubbing alcohol

- Water

- Cotton swab

- Hair dryer

- Sponge

- Large glass or plastic sealable storage container

TIME REQUIRED: 1 HOUR

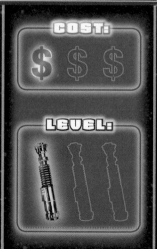

COST:
$ $ $

LEVEL:

Step 1: Make a solution of rubbing alcohol and water by mixing 1 ounce of alcohol with 4 ounces of water. Dip the cotton in the solution and rub down the three strands of hair, to remove any oils, dirt, or other substances from them. Place the hairs on a clean surface to dry.

Step 2: Cut a triangle of plastic to make the pointer for your hygrometer. The triangle should have a base of about 1 inch and sides of about 2 to 2–½ inches.

Step 3: Use the tape to secure the dime to the sharp point of your triangle. The dime will help stabilize your pointer.

Step 4: Push one nail or thumb-tack through the other end of your triangle, close to the edge. Use the nail to open up a hole slightly larger than the metal so that the triangle will turn freely around it like a board game spinner. Use the glue to attach one end of the hair strands to the center of the triangle, halfway between the dime and the nail. Allow this to dry before continuing.

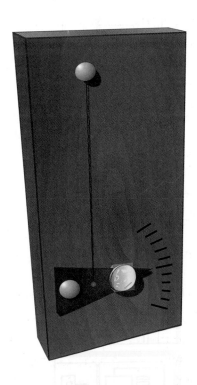

Step 5: Set the wood or Styrofoam on your working surface so you have a tall rectangle. This will serve as the base of your hygrometer. Attach the second nail or thumbtack in the top left corner of your base, about an inch from the top and the side. Then, position your triangle so that the hair attachment is about 6 inches directly below the top nail, and use the nail or thumbtack to attach the triangle to the base.

Step 6: Stretch the hair from the triangle to the nail at the top of the base. Hold the base as though you were hanging it on a wall, and wrap the hair around the nail until it is taut when the triangle is pointing parallel to the floor. If the strands are too long, you may trim them with the scissors. Use the glue to secure the hair to the free nail so the triangle is held in this position. Allow the glue to dry before continuing.

Step 7: You need to determine your scale so it measures from 0 to 100 percent humidity. First, determine the point for 0 percent humidity by gently drying the strands with a hair dryer until the triangle stops moving. Use your marker to place a dot on the base at the point the triangle is pointing to.

To mark your hygrometer for 100 percent humidity, place it in the sealed storage container with a wet sponge or paper towel. Don't let the sponge touch the hygrometer. Check to see the position of the pointer after ten minutes. Continue to let the hygrometer sit in the box, checking it at ten-minute intervals until the pointer stops moving. Mark this spot with your marker. To calibrate your scale, divide the space between the two marks into even intervals. If you can place nine marks between them, each one will represent a change of 10 percent. If you can only fit three or four marks, they will represent changes of 25 or 20 percent, respectively.

Step 8: Your hygrometer is ready to go! Place it in a safe place, where it won't get wet, and observe it over the coming days. Try looking at it at different times of day. Does the pointer move? Make records of your observations and see if any patterns emerge. With a tool like this, you'll be able to determine the best time of day for harvesting water from the atmosphere, whether you're at home or on Tatooine!

THE Secret:

Hair is made up of proteins and cells that can absorb water. The more water the hair absorbs, the longer the cells making up the hair will be. If there's much high humidity, the hair will swell and allow the pointer to drop. When the hair is drier, the protein pulls back and shortens, pulling the pointer upward.

UNDERGROUND COOLING

When Luke enters his home, he descends stairs into an underground building. Like others who inhabit the hot deserts of Tatooine, Luke's family lives beneath the surface of the planet. With the brutal heat of the twin suns, the lack of water and shade, and the harsh desert surface, could there be a practical reason for a subterranean dwelling? Here's how to test if building one's home underground is a good way to beat the heat.

WHAT YOU NEED:

- **2 red alcohol thermometers***
- **2 disposable 1-quart plastic containers**
- **Scissors or a screwdriver**
- **2 aquariums**
- **Sand**
- **A warm, sunny place**

* Scientific-grade red alcohol thermometers with long stems can be purchased online for $3 to $5 a piece.

TIME REQUIRED:
15 MINUTES TO SET UP, AND A DAY TO OBSERVE PERIODICALLY

COST:
$ $ $

LEVEL:
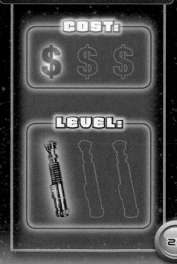

Step 1: Your plastic containers are going to represent your different homes. Using your scissors or screwdriver, make a hole in the bottom of both containers that the thermometers can just fit through. You want a tight fit so the thermometers can be held with the bulbs suspended in the middle of the container. Flip the containers upside down and push the thermometers through from the bottom 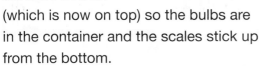 (which is now on top) so the bulbs are in the container and the scales stick up from the bottom.

Step 2: Your model homes will be placed in the aquariums, which will be your deserts. For house #1, place about an inch of sand in one aquarium, and then place one of the plastic containers upside down in the middle of the tank so the thermometer is sticking up.

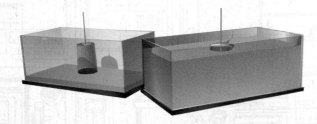

Next, add sand to the aquarium until the container is fully covered. The thermometer should be sticking up out the sand. If you aren't able to read all of the numbers, you may need to move some of the sand out of the way to read the temperature, which is fine.

For house #2, place a few inches of sand in the second aquarium. The second container will be positioned upside down on top of the sand in this setup. You can push the edges of the container into the sand about an inch to hold it in place.

Step 3: Find a warm and sunny spot where you can leave your desert homes for the day. If the weather isn't cooperating, you can also use two hot desk lamps, one pointed at each setup, to approximate the effect of the sun. (Make sure the lightbulbs in the lamps are of the same wattage so you have, ideally, similar situations.) Make a note of the starting temperatures, which should be about the same. Throughout the day, check your thermometers and see if the temperatures of the two homes are changing. Are they changing in the same way? If you had to build a home on Tatooine, which approach do you think you would use?

CREATING A LAVA LAMP

The planet Mustafar is a dangerous place covered with flowing lava. The Separatist hideout is where Jedi Master Obi-Wan Kenobi must confront and destroy his former apprentice, Anakin Skywalker, who becomes the Sith Lord Darth Vader. Molten rock isn't a substance one can work with easily (nor would you want to!), but it's not too hard to make a "lava lamp" that gives the appearance of flowing just like the lava on the surface of Mustafar.

WHAT YOU NEED:

TIME REQUIRED: 15 MINUTES

- Empty plastic bottle, 1 or 2 liters work well

- Vegetable oil

- Water

- Food coloring

- Effervescent antacid tablets

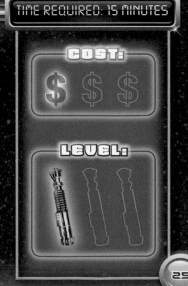

COST:

$ $ $

LEVEL:

Step 1: Fill the plastic bottle with oil, leaving about three or four inches of space at the top.

Step 2: Add water to the bottle until it's almost filled to the neck.

Step 3: Choose a color for your lava. Red would make sense, but any color will have a nice effect. Add 10 to 20 drops of food coloring to the bottle, more for a 2-liter bottle, less for a smaller bottle.

Step 4: Open your antacid tablets and break them into quarters. You'll want to use one tablet for each liter your bottle can hold. Add the tablet pieces to the bottle quickly and stand back to watch the lava start to bubble up!

You can try different-sized bottles or colors with your lamps. When the lava stops bubbling, feel free to repeat Step 4 as many times as you like to start the "lamp" up again.

THE Secret:

You may have heard that water and oil don't mix. So when you have colored water in oil, the two liquids will stay separate. The water is denser and collects naturally below the oil in a container, but when you add an antacid tablet, the bubbles that form, which are carbon dioxide, push the water up as they rise. The water will sink to the bottom again but any bubbling will continue to send it to the top. When you combine oil, colored water, and an antacid: Voilà! A magic oil bubbler!

MAKING ICICLES

Before Luke Skywalker can make it back to the Rebel base on Hoth, he is attacked by a vicious wampa. The brutal beast drags Luke back to its cave. When Luke wakes up, he finds himself suspended upside down from a ceiling dripping with huge icicles. How exactly do icicles form? That's just what you can find out with this activity.

WHAT YOU NEED:

- 6-ounces of water
- Weather with temperatures below freezing (or access to a freezer)
- 7- or 8-ounce paper cup
- 5-ounce paper cup
- Pin or needle
- Paper towel
- Large, clear plastic cup with a mouth larger than the bottom of the 5-ounce cup
- Pencil
- Index card
- Scissors
- Masking tape

TIME REQUIRED:
15 MINUTES ACTIVE,
AND 1-1/2 TO 2 HOURS
FREEZING TIME

COST:
$ $ $

LEVEL:

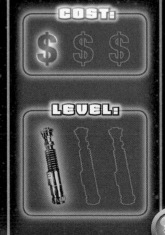

27

WHAT TO DO:

Step 1: Use the pin or needle to make a small hole in the bottom of the 7- or 8-ounce paper cup and cover the hole on the outside of the cup with masking tape. Fill this cup ¾ full with water and place it in the freezer or out in the cold for 30 to 60 minutes. If the weather is below 30 degrees Fahrenheit, you can use the outdoors. Just be sure to place the cup somewhere out of the sun.

Step 2: Use the pencil to make three evenly spaced holes in the bottom of the 5-ounce paper cup. Use the scissors to cut a piece of paper towel that will snugly line the bottom of the cup. Put the circle of paper towel in the cup and use the pencil to gently push

the towel into each of the three holes. The towel needs to just barely reach below the bottom of the cup.

Step 3: Use the pencil to trace the bottom of the smaller cup onto the center of the index card. Fold the card in half and cut a hole a little larger than the bottom of your cup by cutting a little way outside of the pencil line.

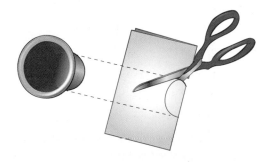

Place the card over the mouth of the clear plastic cup and position your smaller cup (with the paper towel in the hole) so it's held up with 2 or 3 inches of cup hanging down below the index card. If the hole isn't big enough,

cut it a little wider. You want at least 4 or 5 inches between the bottom of the paper cup and plastic cup.

Step 4: After your water has been in the cold for at least 30 minutes (closer to an hour may be better), remove the cup from the freezer. Peel 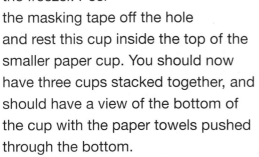 the masking tape off the hole and rest this cup inside the top of the smaller paper cup. You should now have three cups stacked together, and should have a view of the bottom of the cup with the paper towels pushed through the bottom.

Step 5: Put your stack of cups back in the cold. If you're able to use the outdoors, you can check on the setup periodically and see how it has changed. If you're using a freezer,

give the cup at least an hour before you check on it. The longer you leave the cups in the cold, the larger your icicles will be.

Curious about some variations? See what happens if you don't use the paper towel. Or try adding color to the ice. If you add flavoring or juice, you could even make a fun and refreshing bite to eat on a hot day!

KEEPING WARM IN THE COLD

Luke manages to escape the wampa on Hoth, but between his injuries and the blizzard, he doesn't make it far. When Han finds him, Luke has life-threatening hypothermia. Hypothermia (an abnormally low body temperature) can be prevented by keeping someone warm, or reversed by getting their temperature back to normal. Han makes interesting use of his dead tauntaun to save Luke, but materials we have easy access to can also protect against the cold. In this experiment, you'll test a variety of fabrics to see which would be the best in a fight against freezing weather.

WHAT YOU NEED:

- **1- or 2-liter plastic bottle**

- **Water**

- **One-hole stopper to fit the top of the bottle**

- **Red alcohol thermometer**

- **Glycerin or vegetable oil**

- **Notebook and pencil**

- **Clock or stopwatch**

- **Various materials for insulation, such as:**

  - Cotton blanket or clothing
  - Down comforter or jacket
  - Wool blanket or clothing
  - Tank with warm or cold water in it
  - Fiberglass*
  - Fleece blanket or clothing
  - Nylon material

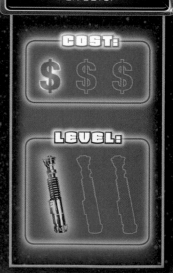

TIME REQUIRED: 30 TO 60 MINUTES PER SETUP

COST:
$ $ $

LEVEL:

* Fiberglass is an irritant, and work gloves should always be worn when handling it. Be very careful to keep its fibers away from your face.

WHAT TO DO:

Step 1: Put a small amount of vegetable oil or glycerin on your fingers and rub this on the bottom of the thermometer. This will enable the glass thermometer to move through the hole in the stopper without sticking and breaking. Using a twisting motion, push the thermometer into the hole in the stopper so the bulb will be in the middle of the bottle when the stopper is in place.

Step 2: Your plastic bottle is going to represent a human body. Since the human body's average temperature rests around 98.6 degrees Fahrenheit, fill the bottle with warm water that reads around 100 degrees Fahrenheit on your thermometer. Warmer water is fine, but you'll want to start with the same temperature water each time. Another option is to ask an adult to help you boil water. Fill the bottle halfway with tap water and then the rest of the way with boiled water. With this technique you can be sure to start with approximately the same

temperature water each time. Make sure the adult pours the hot water for you after it has stopped actively boiling (stopped making bubbles). If the temperature is too hot or too cold, adjust the quantities of boiled and tap water to get closer to 100 degrees.

Step 3: Put the stopper into the bottle, sealing off the top and trapping the water and heat inside. Adjust the position of the thermometer if necessary.

Step 4: Choose which material you will test first and lay it in front of you. Read the temperature on the thermometer. Record this as your starting temperature, then make a note of the time, or start your stopwatch. Carefully wrap the whole bottle in the material of your choice, being especially cautious when covering the thermometer.

Step 5: At ten-minute intervals, move the material away from the thermometer and take a new reading. Make a note of this temperature and time in your notebook. Continue taking readings until the thermometer reads 75 degrees, a fatally low core body temperature.

Step 6: When you've completed your readings for one material,

choose a new material to test. Repeat Steps 2 to 5 for each material you want to test. You could even try using yourself as insulation! Find a way to wrap your body around the bottle, leaving as little of the bottle exposed as possible.

After you've collected data for several materials, compare your results. Is there one material that's clearly best for keeping out the cold? Are there other materials you could try? You could also try a variation on this experiment by repeating the procedure after wetting each of the materials, to see what impact water has on a material's ability to trap heat. After this, you'll be thoroughly prepared to pack for your next cold-weather outing!

PHASES OF THE MOON

Galaxies are filled with moons — large bodies that orbit around larger planets. In the *Star Wars* universe, moons are a common sight, with some planets orbited by more than one. One example is the forest moon of Endor — the home of the friendly and furry Ewoks, and the body over which the second Death Star is constructed. Since moons are essentially large rocks that do not create their own light, what is it that makes them visible to us? It turns out that it takes a sun to see a moon. In this activity, you'll create a device that can model just how our moon and its different phases are illuminated by a light source.

WHAT YOU NEED:

TIME REQUIRED: 1 HOUR

- Shoebox with a lid

- Black paint and paintbrush, or black construction paper

- Small Styrofoam ball, 1" to 2" in diameter

- Black thread

- Glue

- Scissors and/or box cutter*

- Flashlight

- Pencil or marker

- Modeling clay or masking tape

- Notebook

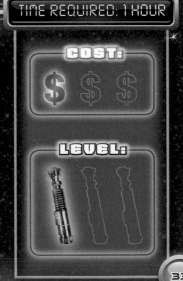

COST:

$ $ $

LEVEL:

* A box cutter is a sharp tool and should be handled with great care or with the help of an adult.

WHAT TO DO:

Step 1:   The inside of your shoebox will be the night sky, so you want it to be black. Use the construction paper and scissors, or the black paint to cover all the inside surfaces of your shoebox with black. Let the paint dry before you continue.

Step 2:   The Styrofoam ball will hang in the middle of the shoebox and act as your moon. Cut a short piece of black thread, about 2 inches. Glue (or tape) one end of the thread to the Styrofoam ball and the other to the middle of the underside of the shoebox lid, so that the "moon" hangs halfway between the floor and ceiling of the shoebox. Allow the glue to dry.

Step 3:   Turn the shoebox so one of the shorter sides is facing you. Place the bulb end of the flashlight against the center of the box's shorter side. Use your pencil to trace on the

box around the flashlight. Then use your scissors or box cutter to cut around the circle you just drew. This will allow the light from the flashlight to illuminate your moon.

Step 4:   Now you'll make smaller holes for viewing your moon from various positions that will represent different phases. The holes should all be at the same level as the moon when it hangs from the top of the box. Cut three holes on the long sides, one about an inch in from each corner, and one in the middle. Place one in the middle of the short side, opposite the flashlight, and place one as close to the flashlight as possible. Use your pencil or marker to number the holes, starting with 1 on the side with the flashlight, and increasing as you move.

Step 5: Position the flashlight so it will stay pointed into the large hole. Use masking tape or modeling clay to hold it in place. Or you can use books or blocks to prop it up.

Step 6: Turn on the flashlight and observe the moon from each of the viewing holes. In your notebook, record your observations by indicating the number of the hole and sketching the way the Styrofoam ball is illuminated. Each view represents a position of the moon relative to the sun as it revolves around the Earth. The light of the sun only illuminates the part of the moon that faces it — how much of that we see from Earth determines the moon's phases.

You can take this further by experimenting on the effect of placing objects, perhaps representing the Earth, between the flashlight and the Styrofoam ball. Can you mimic the effect of an eclipse? What if you put the moon between the Earth and the sun? Now that you have your moon box set up, there's no limit to what you can try with it.

WATER IN THE DESERT

It seems strange that Luke and his family are able to collect moisture from a planet as dry as Tatooine. Deserts are harsh and dangerous places with hardly a drop of water to be found. So how is this possible? Even the driest deserts have more to them than meets the eye. With a little ingenuity, it's possible to show water emerging from the strangest of places.

WHAT YOU NEED:

TIME REQUIRED:
10 MINUTES TO SET UP,
SEVERAL HOURS TO OBSERVE

- Aquarium

- Sand

- Small rocks or other heavy objects

- Clear plastic, like cellophane

- Small plastic container

- Hot lamp

- Small plants like grass, clover, small dandelions

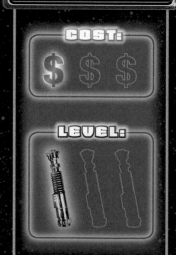

COST:

$ $ $

LEVEL:

WHAT TO DO:

Step 1: In this experiment you're going to design a model desert and see if you can collect any moisture from it. To create your desert, fill the the aquarium with sand so that it is an inch or two deeper than your plastic container.

Step 2: In the center of the aquarium, nestle the plastic container into the sand so that its edges are just below the level of the surface of the sand. Try to prevent sand from falling into your container.

Step 3: Cover the container with the plastic, and use the small rocks to hold the plastic in place. Put just enough sand on top of the plastic so that it sags over the container in the center. If you need to create a little slack in the plastic in order for it to sag by adjusting the rocks, go ahead and do that. You don't need much of an indentation, just a place that's clearly lower than the rest.

Step 4: Position the lamp so it shines onto the sand in the aquarium, and turn it on. Check at 5- to 10-minute intervals to see if any moisture has collected on the plastic or in the container.

Step 5: You can also test whether the presence of plants in your desert impacts the quantity of water that's produced. Remove the plastic from the aquarium and carefully position your small plants as though they are growing around the plastic container. Reposition the plastic, secure it with the small rocks, and use the sand to make a depression in the center. Turn on the light again and make a new set of observations. Is there any difference in how much moisture was collected from the sand without plants?

DESERT LIFE: THE SCIENCE OF SURVIVAL

Life in a desert ecosystem isn't easy. Animals and plants that are successful in the desert have special adaptations that allow them to survive. For animals, this usually includes special ways to rid their bodies of heat, like big ears on elephants or the thick outer shell of a scorpion. On the other hand, plants don't give off heat — but their leaves (or total lack of them) — can prevent excessive water loss in hot climates. Follow this experiment to discover how.

WHAT YOU NEED:

- Paper towels
- Scissors
- Bowl of water
- Wax paper
- Clear tape
- Paper clips
- Pipe cleaners or wire coat hangers
- Clay
- Baking sheet
- Hot lamp or a sunny spot

TIME REQUIRED:
30 TO 45 MINUTES TO SET UP, 24 HOURS TO LET SIT, 15 MINUTES FOR OBSERVATIONS

COST:
$ $ $

LEVEL:

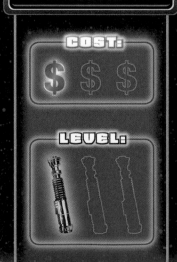

WHAT TO DO:

Step 1: You're going to build three frames for your model plants. First, you'll build the frame using either pipe cleaners or wire coat hangers. Your first two frames should be simple plant stems with three branches each. The third frame should be a wider, cactus-like frame with one or two stems. Your plants can be as tall as you like, but one foot will work well.

Step 2: Use the clay to stand each plant frame on the baking tray so they are evenly spaced.

Step 3: The paper towels will represent the water-bearing parts of the plants — namely the leaves or, in the case of a cactus, the stem.

For plant model #1, use your scissors to cut leaf-shaped pieces of paper towel to hang on the wire stem. Each leaf should be about 3 inches tall and wide; the exact shape isn't important. For each leaf, bend a paper clip to form a double-ended hook, and push one end of the hook through the top of that leaf. Dip each leaf in the bowl of water, and hang it on the stem.

Plant model #2 will have succulent leaves. This means the leaves will be thicker than normal leaves, and have a waxy coating like you would find on an aloe plant. For each of these leaves, fold a whole paper towel into as small a square as possible and dip it in the bowl of water. Wrap this folded square in a single layer of wax paper. Then use your scissors to cut the wax paper to the appropriate size, and use the tape to secure the wax paper around the paper towel. Do this for each leaf. Once again, use the paper clips to make hooks to hang each leaf on your model stem.

Plant model #3 will represent a cactus. The stem of this plant will be very thick; there will be no actual leaves, and the whole plant will be covered by a waxy coating. For this plant, dip full paper towels in the water and wrap them around the wire base of the cactus.

Continue to layer on paper towels until the body of your cactus is more than an inch thick. You can make the cactus as thick as you like. When your stem is thick enough, use the wax paper and tape to fully cover the outside of the cactus.

Step 4: Put your plants in a bright, warm place (a sunny window would be perfect), and let them sit for 24 hours.

Step 5: After 24 hours have passed, examine the paper towels in each plant model. For the plants representing aloe, #2, and a cactus, #3, unwrap the wax paper and check the water content of the paper inside. Which of the three plant models held its water the best? Which one seems to have dried out the most? Given your observations, what are at least two characteristics that are likely to be found in successful desert plants?

DRESSING FOR HOT WEATHER

Tusken Raiders are covered from head to toe in desert-colored rags and robes, leaving no bare skin exposed to the elements. These beings have lived in the desert for generations and know the best ways to stay cool, comfortable, and protected from the intense heat of the sun. But have you ever wondered why so many desert dwellers seem to choose long, flowing robes over tight-fitting, closely cropped outfits? In this experiment, you'll compare different outfits and determine which would be best for life in the desert.

WHAT YOU NEED:

- **2 full-length, loose-fitting robes with hoods** — one light in color, one dark

- **2 pairs of lightweight, long pants that fit close to the skin** — one light, one dark

- **2 lightweight long-sleeve shirts that fit close to the skin** — one light, one dark

- **Notebook and pencil**

- **Water bottle**

- **Watch**

- **Several hot and sunny days, preferably with low humidity**

- **A place to walk**

TIME REQUIRED: 1 HOUR FOR EACH OUTFIT, PROBABLY OVER THE COURSE OF SEVERAL DAYS

COST: $ $ $

LEVEL: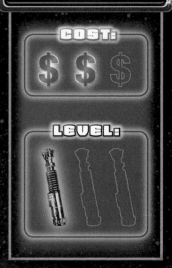

Note: Clothing material matters! Whatever you choose, make sure you're consistent. We recommend using a wool, especially for the robes, or a lightweight wool or wicking fabric for the pants and shirts. Beware of cotton! It absorbs water and doesn't let it evaporate easily.

Unfortunately, several important factors affecting your results will be difficult to control in this experiment. The best weather for your test is that which approximates the weather in a desert: hot and dry, perhaps with a breeze. If you live somewhere with weather like this, then you're in good shape. If not, you may need to work on this experiment on several occasions over a number of days or weeks. Hot but humid weather will give you different results that are still interesting, but do not reflect true desert conditions. Do your best to find a set of days when the weather will be hot, dry, and sunny.

Step 1: On a day when the weather is close to the conditions you're looking for, choose which of the FOUR outfits you will try first, and get dressed.

(1) Pair the light robe with minimal clothing underneath the fabric (underwear and a tank top at most)

(2) Pair the dark robe with minimal clothing underneath the fabric (underwear and a tank top at most)

(3) Pair the light pants with the light shirt.

(4) Pair the dark pants with the dark shirt. Determine where you can take a leisurely walk, perhaps around your neighborhood or maybe just around the local track. Set your notebook up for data collection by making a page for each walk. Label the page with the outfit you chose, the time of day you're walking, and the weather conditions and temperature when you depart. Create headings for columns on the page where you can make notes about anything you think you might want to make

observations regarding. (See sample chart on next page.)

Step 2: With your notebook, pencil, and water bottle, hit the pavement for a leisurely 30- to 60-minute walk. While you're walking, make note of how your body feels in the clothes you're wearing. How quickly do you get hot? Is sweat building up and wetting the clothing? How quickly do you feel thirsty? Can you feel air moving on your skin, or do you simply feel hot? Make notes of the time when you notice different aspects of your comfort change.

Make sure to drink lots of water if you're thirsty. If you feel overly tired or dizzy, get yourself somewhere cool and shady to rest. You shouldn't be out in the heat or exerting yourself enough to make you unwell. If you start to feel unwell, it's time to take a break.

Step 3: When you've finished your walk, look over your notes and see if there's anything you'd like to add. What was the experience like overall? Did the outfit feel comfortable?

Step 4: Repeat Steps 1 to 3 with the other outfits. For a more complete set of data, see if anyone else will participate in the experiment. If you have more than one set of each outfit, you can have several people walking together at once. The more people who try the outfits and add to your observations, the more significant your results will be.

Step 5: Once you've collected all your data, look over your results. Did one outfit seem to keep people the coolest? What difference did the color of the fabric make? Was there agreement between different people about which outfit was the best? If you had to move through the desert in the heat of the day, how would you dress to prepare?

	Sweat	Comfort	Thirst	Energy Level	Air Movement
Light robe					
Dark robe					
Light pants/light shirt					
Dark pants/dark shirt					

THE Secret:

The clothing one wears in the desert directly affects one's comfort. Fully covering the skin is an important part of protecting oneself from the damaging rays of the sun. But after that, the color and fit of the fabric can make a big difference. Dark clothes attract the light of the sun and can absorb more heat, making fitted, dark clothes less comfortable than lightly colored ones. But loose-fitting robes allow air to circulate against the skin, which helps sweat evaporate and, in turn, helps us cool off.

People who spend a lot of time out and about in the desert heat usually opt for loose-fitting robes due to the impact of the air circulation. As for whether the robes are light or dark in color, as long as the fabric is thick enough, the heat won't be transferred from the fabric to the person's skin, so choosing a light or dark fabric is more about environment and culture. Turbans aren't loose fitting, but the fabric is wrapped thick enough that the head is protected from the heat of the sun, which keeps the body cooler.

SOUND IN SPACE

Starfighters screeching and lasers noisily blasting through space are common sounds in the *Star Wars* universe. But in real space, would you be able to hear these sounds, or is it all part of the movie magic? In this experiment, you'll learn how sound travels differently through air, liquid, and solid matter, and gain some insight into the seemingly noisy confrontations in outer space.

WHAT YOU NEED:

TIME REQUIRED: 1 HOUR

- A partner

- 2 notebooks and pencils

- 2 empty tin cans with no top on one side, empty soup cans work well

- Hammer and nail

- Measuring tape

- Heavy-duty string, at least 20 or 30 yards long and about the same thickness as the nail

- Access to a pool or a still body of water, the quieter the better

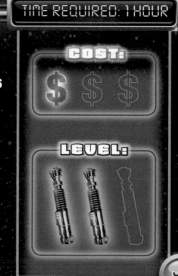

COST:
$ $ $

LEVEL:

47

WHAT TO DO:

Preparation: You're going to do three trials: (1) in the air, (2) using a tin-can phone as a solid, and (3) in the water.

Either you or your partner will say words at different distances and the other person will need to determine what word was said. Whoever will be doing the speaking should come up with *three different lists* of 8 words each (for a total of 24 different words). Don't let the person who will be doing the listening see the words yet. Identify which list will be spoken in the air, into the tin can, and in the water.

EXPERIMENT #1:

Step 1: The first test is the easiest. Stand about 18 inches from your partner and have the person speaking say the first word. The word should be spoken in a normal tone and volume, as should every word spoken in the experiment. Whoever is doing the listening should record the word that was spoken in his notebook.

Step 2: Move through the first list of 8 words, using a new word each time as you reposition yourself at a distance of 1 yard, 5 yards, 10 yards, 15 yards, 20 yards, 25 yards, and 30 yards. Remember, each word should be spoken at the same volume as all the others. The listener should record what he hears at each distance.

EXPERIMENT #2:

Step 1: Using your second list of 8 words, go to a pool and repeat experiment #1 with your mouth and ears submerged. The notebooks can be held in your hands above the water while you conduct the test.

EXPERIMENT #3:

Step 1: Make your tin-can phone. Use the hammer and nail to make a small hole in the bottom of the two cans. Thread the end of the string into the mouth of one can and through the bottom, and continue to thread into the bottom of the second can. It's important that the string be snug in the hole without much space around its edges. Pull the string far enough out of the second can so that you can tie a knot in the end that will prevent

the string from pulling back through the can bottom. When you're finished, you should have the string connecting the two cans with their bottoms facing each other, and the ball of remaining string sticking out of the open end of the first can. This will allow you to lengthen your phone for each trial.

Step 2: Using your third list of 8 words, repeat experiments #1, but the speaker should hold his can over his mouth and say the words into it. The listener should hold his can over his ear.

Final step: Compare the list of words to what the listener heard and wrote down. Examine your results. See how many words the listener was accurately able to hear under each of the circumstances.

Was there one situation that allowed the person to hear the clearest? Was there one situation where the sound clearly didn't travel as well as the other two?

THE Secret:

Consider the nature of matter. All matter is made up of molecules. In solids (the cans and string), the molecules are tightly packed together. In liquids (the water), the molecules are looser. And in gasses (the air), the molecules are able to move around and spread out freely. In which type of matter did the sound move the best? The worst?

Now consider how sound travels. It travels in waves by making molecules vibrate. In order for sound to be heard, molecules must be present. But in the middle of space, out of the atmosphere of planets and other large objects, there is nothing but a vacuum. That means there are no molecules whatsoever. Think about your results from this experiment and apply this to the situation in outer space. Do you think spaceships would make audible noises? Would lasers be heard as they fire? On the other hand, would any scene with starfighters be as much fun if you couldn't hear them flying? The answer, sadly, is no.

BUILD A MAGNETOMETER

Magnetic fields allow space travellers to breathe comfortably without the fear of being sucked into open space through an open hangar door. Here on Earth we also have a magnetic field, which protects us. Sometimes, storms on the sun can send blasts of radiation our way that affect the Earth's magnetic field. This activity will show you how to build a magnetometer, a tool used to monitor Earth's magnetic field. Then you can see for yourself just what kind of impact sun storms have here on our planet.

WHAT YOU NEED:

- **Clear 2-liter plastic bottle – labels removed**

- **Scissors, ruler, glue, pencil**

- **Plastic straw**

- **Index card**

- **Craft mirror, ½" to 1" in diameter***

- **Small bar magnet****

- **Sand**

- **Clear packing tape**

- **Hammer and nail**

- **Thread**

- **High-intensity desk lamp**

- **Large white poster board or drafting paper**

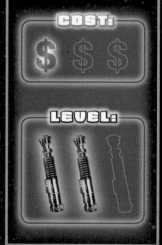

TIME REQUIRED:
1 HOUR TO ASSEMBLE,
AT LEAST ONE WEEK FOR
OBSERVATIONS

COST:
$ $ $

LEVEL:

---

* Craft mirrors can be purchased inexpensively from craft stores or online retailers.

**Bar magnets can be purchased online. Choose a magnet that is 2" long at most and no more than ¼" to ½" thick.

Step 1: Cut the 2-liter bottle in two horizontally, about 4 inches from the top. Use the hammer and nail to make a small hole in the center of the cap. Fill the bottom of the bottle with several inches of sand to weigh the device down when it's completed.

Step 2: Trim the index card using the scissors into a rectangle that fits easily inside the bottle with room to move freely. Use the ruler to measure a 2-inch section of straw and cut this with the scissors.

Step 3: Glue the mirror to the center of the card with the reflecting surface facing out. Then glue the magnet to the card directly above the mirror, horizontally, and glue the straw horizontally directly above the magnet.

Step 4: Use the ruler and scissors to measure and cut two pieces of thread: one 8 inches long, and the other 6 inches long. Thread the 8-inch piece through the straw and tie the two ends together to form a triangle with 2-inch sides. Tie one end of the 6-inch piece to the top of this triangle.

Step 5: Take the top piece of the plastic bottle (with the cap in place) and position the index card inside the bottle. Thread the free end of the 6-inch thread through the top of the bottle and through the hole in the bottle cap.

Step 6: Put the two pieces of plastic bottle back together and reconnect them using the clear packing tape. Adjust the length of thread hanging from the top so the index card hangs freely, with the mirror several inches below the seam in the bottle. Use the glue to secure the string in place and keep the height of the mirror constant.

This is your magnetometer

Experiment with the position of your magnetometer and light until you have a clear reflection of light from the index card onto the white paper. Allow the magnetometer to settle so there is no movement in the card, and use a pencil to mark the reflection on the white paper. Either number this spot with a 1 and record the date in a notebook, or put the date directly onto the white paper.

Step 7: Find a large table against a wall or a place in a room where your magnetometer can remain undisturbed for the period of time over which you would like to make observations. (We recommend taking readings for at least a week.) Place the white paper against the wall (preferably facing east or west) and use tape to secure its position. Place the magnetometer 5 or 6 feet from the wall with the mirror on the index card facing the wall. Position the lamp so it will shine directly on the mirror without blocking the light reflected back at the wall.

Over the course of the next week, check the position of the reflection on the wall. Check at least once a day, but several times a day is even better. Whenever the reflection is in a new spot, mark this and date it with the pencil. Make sure that neither the light nor the magnetometer are shifted or moved in any way over the time when you are making your observations. If the equipment is repositioned even a fraction of an inch, it will impact your results. (If you can turn off the lamp without touching it, from a wall switch or power strip, do this between observations to save energy. Just make certain you do not move the lamp as it could change results.)

THE Secret:

You should be able to observe several positions of the reflection over time. Earth's magnetic field affects the magnet on your card and shifts its orientation relative to Earth. This is evident in the shift in the reflection. This magnetic field is fairly constant, but solar storms send charged particles and radiation from the sun that can cause subtle shifts in the field to occur. Now you have a tool that can tell you just when these storms are occurring and can show how forceful their impact is here on Earth.

PART II
SIGNS OF THE FORCE

STAYING FOCUSED

When Luke goes to Dagobah to train with Yoda, he's determined to become a Jedi. Yoda is at first reluctant to take him as a pupil, but Obi-Wan's spirit convinces the Jedi Master that Luke is a worthy apprentice. Despite his desire to succeed, Luke struggles to perform the more difficult tasks that Yoda sets before him. His mind wanders, his focus dwindles, and he meets failure again and again. Just how easy is it to distract the human brain? Use this test and you may find that Luke isn't the only one who is easily distracted.

WHAT YOU NEED:

- **4 or more pieces of poster board or white construction paper**
- **At least 6 colored markers**
- **Stopwatch**
- **Notebook and pencil**

- **Calculator**
- **Graph paper**
- **Willing subjects**

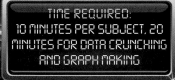

TIME REQUIRED:
10 MINUTES PER SUBJECT, 20 MINUTES FOR DATA CRUNCHING AND GRAPH MAKING

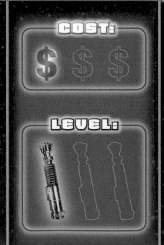

COST:
$ $ $

LEVEL:

WHAT TO DO:

Step 1: Create your tests as follows. You will want at least three different tests, each on a piece of construction paper or poster board cut to approximately 8 x 10 inches or larger. On the first piece of paper, use each of your markers to write the name of the color of the marker. Use letters that are at least an inch tall and space the color names evenly from the top to the bottom of the paper. Each word should be the color of the ink it's written in.

On the second piece of paper, write the color names again, but this time only write the first and last letters of the word in the color of the ink. Write the rest of the name in a different color. On the third piece of paper, write each name in a color different from its own ink. If you like, you can create a fourth test with three different inks used in each of the color names.

Step 2: On a clean piece of paper, create a model test to introduce your subjects to the activity. Write two or three different color names using any of the techniques from your official tests.

Step 3: Set up a data table to record your observations. Create one column for the subjects and a column for each of the tests. Divide each test column into two and put the headings TIME and MISTAKES at the top of the two smaller columns. Create a row for each person you will test. Label the row at the bottom of your table AVERAGE.

Step 4: Determine who will take your tests. One at a time and in a place where your other subject won't be able to see what you're doing, administer the challenge. Have your subjects enter the room to find the three or four tests face-down on a table where they can sit. The tests should be arranged in no particular order. The subjects will need to turn over a test paper and tell you what color ink each word is written in. Use the sample test you created to explain the activity and practice the assignment once or twice with the words you've written on the sample card. When the person is ready, clear the stopwatch and tell them to begin.

For each test, count how many mistakes the person makes and use the stop-watch to determine the length of time needed to complete each page. Record this information in your data table.

Step 5: Once you've administered the test to at least four people, calculate the average time needed to take each test and the average number of mistakes made on each test. You can do this by adding the numbers in a column and dividing that sum by the number of subjects you tested. Record your averages in the last row of your table.

Step 6: Use your graph paper to create a bar graph of your results. Write the tests along the bottom of the graph (this is your x-axis). Along the left-hand side, write MISTAKES in one color and TIME (SEC) in another. Make a scale along this side for each unit (this is your y-axis). You might be able to use one box for each mistake and one for each second of time. If your numbers are too big, try making each box represent more mistakes or seconds. If you have plenty of room, consider using two or three boxes for each mistake or second.

Above each test name, fill in the boxes that correspond with the average time used and mistakes made with the color you used to write the unit on the axis. This should give you a clear picture of the impact of combining different ink and names on a person's accuracy. How easily distracted were people by the words? Can you think of ways to change the test to add distraction? You could use music or a flashing light somewhere in the room and see if additional stimuli cause any further distractions.

USING INVISIBLE FORCES

The Force is a powerful ally to the Jedi, who can accomplish amazing feats by tapping into it. One of those feats is to move objects without actually touching them, like reaching a dropped lightsaber, or pushing an enemy away during battle. But the Jedi aren't the only ones who can use invisible forces to make objects move or defy gravity. Here are three methods that will have others believing that you can tap into the Force, too.

WHAT YOU NEED:

TIME REQUIRED:
EXPERIMENT #1 TAKES
20 MINUTES, EXPERIMENTS
#2 AND #3 TAKE 5 MINUTES

EXPERIMENT #1:

- **Modeling clay or small Styrofoam square at least ½" thick**
- **Flexible drinking straw or other, non-conductive, L-shaped object**
- **Tissue paper**
- **Tape, scissors, ruler**
- **Clear, thick plastic, like a report folder**
- **Printer paper or wool blanket or sweater**
- **Cellophane**

EXPERIMENT #2:

- **Plastic comb**
- **Dry hair of medium or long length**
- **A tap or water spigot**

EXPERIMENT #3:

- **Drinking glass**
- **Water**
- **Index card or small cardboard square that completely covers the mouth of the glass**

COST:

$ $ $

LEVEL:

EXPERIMENT #1: Make an electroscope to detect static electricity.

Step 1: Build your demonstration setup. Make a base with a small ball of the modeling clay or with a square of Styrofoam. Press the long end of the straw or other L-shaped object into the base so it stands straight up. If you're using a straw, bend the short end so it is at a 90-degree angle to the long side.

Step 2: Cut a rectangle of tissue paper that is approximately 1 inch by 8 inches and fold it in half. Hang the tissue paper over the short arm of your base so half hangs on each side, and use a small piece of tape to secure it at the top.

Step 3: Cut a square from the clear plastic that measures about 4 inches on a side. With the printer paper or wool on a table, rub the plastic square against it for about 10 seconds.

Step 4: Slowly bring the plastic closer to the outside of the tissue paper without letting the two touch, and watch what happens. Try this on both sides of the setup. After you've done this a few times, let the tissue paper and the plastic touch and repeat the beginning of this step.

Step 5: Rub the plastic on the printer paper or wool for another ten seconds and this time bring the plastic between the two sheets without touching them. Observe what happens. What happens when you do let the plastic and the paper touch?

EXPERIMENT #2: Bend water without touching it.

Step 1: Turn on the water lightly, so it leaves the tap flowing in a narrow stream. The stream should be continuous but as small as possible.

Step 2: Run the comb through the hair for 10 to 20 seconds.

Step 3: Slowly bring the comb close to the water stream and observe what happens.

EXPERIMENT #3: Water that defies the laws of gravity.

Step 1: Fill the cup with water so it is full or almost full. Place the index card or cardboard so it covers the mouth of the cup, and hold it in place.

Step 2: This step should be practiced outside, over a sink, or in the shower where it will be okay if you spill. Carefully, with your hand holding the index card in place, invert the cup so it is completely upside down. Try doing this at different speeds to see the best way to invert the cup without spilling any water. You may need to try this a few times before it works well.

Step 3: Carefully release the pressure holding the index card to the cup. Once you get the hang of this, amaze your family and friends by showing them how you can use the Force to make water defy gravity!

THE Secret:

Experiments #1 and #2: Electricity (whether it's static or powering your lights) is generated by the movement of charged particles. There are negatively and positively charged particles. The two different types attract each other, but repel particles with the same charge. When you rub the plastic on the paper or wool, negative particles build up in the square. When the plastic is then brought near the paper, the negative charges attract the positive charges in the tissue paper toward them. When the two touch, the negative charges balance out, which cause them to push each other away. Negative charges build up in the comb when you put it through hair, and those particles attract positive charges in the water, causing the stream to bend.

Experiment #3: Air pressure is the key to this trick. With little or no air in the cup, the pressure of the air outside the cup is greater than that inside. This pressure is enough to hold the index card or cardboard in place and keep the water from spilling out. If the seal between the card and the cup is broken, water will leak out and air will move in. The pressure of this air will be enough to push the water out of the cup and let gravity do its work.

CREATE LIGHTNING

In the world of *Star Wars*, Sith Lords can create Force lightning to cause great pain in their enemies. Force lightning shoots from Emperor Palpatine's fingertips as he battles his opponents, to devastating results. It might seem as if only a Sith Lord can conjure lightning out of nothing, but it's easier than you might think. Here's a way for you to generate your very own little lightning bolts — to good results!

WHAT YOU NEED:

- Disposable foil pie plate, any size
- Pencil with rubber eraser
- Thumbtack (the kind with a flat head, not a pushpin)
- Wool sock
- Styrofoam block or square, about the size of the pie plate
- A dark room

TIME REQUIRED:
20 TO 30 MINUTES

COST:
$ $ $

LEVEL:

Step 1: Push the thumbtack into the foil pie plate from the bottom, so the sharp end sticks up in the middle of the plate when it's right-side up.

Step 2: Push the eraser end of the pencil into the tack so the pencil sticks straight up out of the bottom of the plate. If you want, you can use glue to secure the position of the pencil. Do not touch the metal of the pie plate with your skin from this point on.

Step 3: Rub the sock on the Styrofoam block for 10 to 20 seconds.

Step 4: By holding the pencil, pick up the pie plate and push the bottom into the Styrofoam block so the butt of the tack pushes into the Styrofoam and holds the pie plate in place. The pie plate should lie flat and be in contact

with the Styrofoam when you've finished this step.

Step 5: Turn out the lights and make sure the room is as dark as possible. Bring your hand slowly toward the plate and observe what happens. Can you feel anything before you see something? Is there any noise?

To repeat the experiment, hold the pie plate up by the pencil and rub the sock on the Styrofoam, once again being careful not to touch the foil with your skin until you're ready to make observations. Once you've rubbed the sock on the Styrofoam for 10 to 20 seconds, place the plate back on a tabletop and once again bring your hand slowly toward the foil plate. For a variation, try rubbing the sock directly on the foil plate and see what happens. Are the results the same?

THE Secret:

The lightning produced in this activity is the result of built-up negative charges in the foil jumping to the positive charges in your skin. The charges are transferred to the foil from the wool by way of the Styrofoam. This is the same type of reaction that causes static (which produces sparks on naturally dry days) when you touch a person or metal object after wearing socks on a carpet.

WATCHING AIR PRESSURE

After Vader is nearly killed on Mustafar, the Emperor finds a way to keep him alive, but Vader's destroyed body only survives with the aid of a life-support helmet and armor. Without these aids, Darth Vader must stay in a special airtight medical chamber. How much effect can air pressure have on an object? In this activity, you'll observe just how much force the pressure of air can generate.

WHAT YOU NEED:

- Square metal can (like those used for cooking oil) with a top
- Hot plate or stove*
- ¼ cup water

- Oven mitt or heatproof glove
- Hot pad or heat-resistant surface

TIME REQUIRED:
20 MINUTES

COST:
$ $ $

LEVEL:

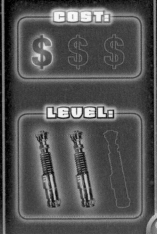

* Make sure you ask an adult to help you when using a stove or hot plate.

WHAT TO DO:

Step 1: Make sure the can is empty and clean. Place the can top where you can find it again in a few minutes. Add about ¼ cup of water to the can. Place the can on the stove or hot plate and bring the water to a boil. Allow steam to leave the can for at least 30 seconds.

Step 2: Using the oven mitt, remove the can from the stove and place it on the hot pad or heat-resistant surface. Carefully put the top back on the can and close it tightly. You may want to use

another oven mitt or glove to handle the top, which may get hot when it comes in contact with the can.

Step 3: Let the can sit and see what happens. You may need to wait for ten or more minutes before the results appear. If you try this a few times and get a sense of how long it takes for the reaction to kick in, you could set up the experiment in secret, position the can, and then invite people to watch you crush the can from across the room using the Force!

THE Secret:

When the can is heated, the air inside expands and leaves the can. If you seal the can while it's still hot, there will be less air inside it than there was before you heated it. This means the pressure of the air inside the can is less than the pressure of the air surrounding it. The force of the external pressure pushing against the can is what causes the can to collapse.

BUILDING A BAROMETER

Did you know air has weight? As gravity pulls it toward the Earth, air puts pressure on everything beneath it — this is called air pressure. Different places have different air pressures depending on the force of gravity and the quantity of air in the atmosphere above where a measurement is taken. For instance, the pressure on the surface of a large planet is greater than that on the surface of a small one. In outer space, there's no air pressure at all. The pressure of air in a given place is changing almost constantly depending on the qualities of the air. A barometer is a tool that scientists use to measure and detect changes in air pressure. Here's how to build your own barometer so you can monitor the changes in air pressure in your own home.

WHAT YOU NEED:

- Balloon

- Scissors

- Rubber bands

- Knitting needle, long barbeque skewer, or other straight, lightweight, pointed object (at least 10" long)

- Glue

- Glass jar

- Marker

- Paper

- Corkboard and a thumbtack or tape

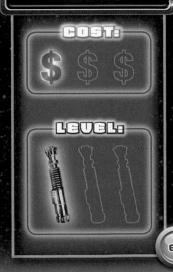

TIME REQUIRED:
10 MINUTES TO SET UP,
SEVERAL DAYS OF
OBSERVATION

COST:

$ $ $

LEVEL:

WHAT TO DO:

Step 1: Cut the long end (that you blow into) off the balloon. Stretch the remaining rubber over the mouth of the jar, and pull it onto the rim until it lies evenly across the top of the jar.

Step 2: On the jar's rim use the rubber bands to secure the position of the balloon.

Step 3: Position the knitting needle (or whichever long object you're using) so the blunt end is in middle of the balloon and the pointed end sticks out about 8 inches past the jar. This will be the pointer of your barometer. Glue the pointer's blunt end to the center of the balloon (see illustration), adding a piece of tape to keep it steady while it dries. When the glue is dry, the pointer should stick straight out from the side of the jar. If you need to, adjust the balloon until the pointer sticks straight out.

Step 4: You need to make a scale for your barometer. Cut a paper rectangle that's about 2 inches wide and 10 inches tall. Make small lines from the top to the bottom with a half inch between each one and evenly spaced smaller lines between these.

Step 5: Find the place you will set up your barometer. You will need to find a surface near or against a wall where you can prop the corkboard (or ask if it's okay to tape the scale directly to the wall). Place the jar against the wall with the pointer sticking straight out to one side. Position the paper so that the pointer matches up with the middle line and attach the paper to the

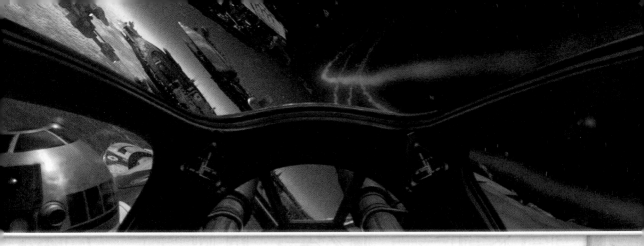

corkboard or wall. Mark this middle line. Use color or a label to indicate that the lines above this point represent high pressure and the lines below this point represent low pressure. If you want to record the pressure changes, assign numbers to the lines, starting with zero at the bottom of the scale.

Step 6: Over the next few days, observe where the needle is pointing. Try observing at different times of day as well. If you're recording your observations, make notes of the time of day as well as the weather conditions when you take your readings. Do you notice any patterns?

THE Secret:

While your barometer can't provide you with actual readings of the air pressure, you can get readings of the pressure relative to the pressure present when you made the barometer. Whatever the pressure was when you sealed off your jar is the pressure inside the jar. As the pressure in the air around the jar changes — a low pressure front moving in with a rainstorm, for example — this will interact with the pressure of the air in the jar. Lower pressure outside the jar allows the air inside the jar to push the balloon up and move the pointer down. If the pressure outside the jar increases, this will push the balloon down into the jar. Try opening and closing the barometer in different kinds of weather and see how this impacts your readings over the next few days. You'll have more dramatic changes depending on how low or high the pressure is when you seal off your jar.

YOUR VERY OWN LIE DETECTOR

Chancellor Palpatine worked with the Republic for years without anyone guessing his true identity as the Sith Lord, Darth Sidious. Not even the Jedi Masters were able to detect his deception until it was too late. Most people are not able to lie so well. There are machines out there that can be used to detect subtle changes in our bodies that reveal when we're telling an untruth. In this experiment, you'll develop a lie-detector test to see if you can hone your skills at catching someone in a lie. If the Jedi had used this test on Palpatine, perhaps things would have gone differently for the Republic.

WHAT YOU NEED:

- **Automatic digital blood pressure monitor***

- **Stethoscope**

- **Stopwatch or clock with a second hand**

- **Paper and pencil**

- **Willing test subjects**

- **A partner****

- **A quiet room with a table and chair**

- **Stopwatch**

*Automatic blood pressure monitors can be purchased online or at some drug stores for approximately $50.

**You can do this experiment without a partner, but in this case you will not use the stethoscope and stopwatch or clock.

TIME REQUIRED: 20 MINUTES TO PREPARE, 20 MINUTES PER TEST SUBJECT

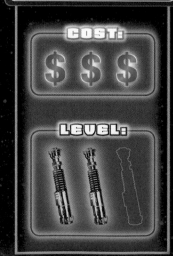

COST:

$ $ $

LEVEL:

WHAT TO DO:

Step 1: Before you begin testing people, make up a list of ten questions you will ask them. The questions should require some explanation on the part of your test subject and not have simple yes or no answers. The longer the answer, the easier it will be for you to collect your data. Questions about life history or personal experiences work well. Keep this list handy so you can refer to it with each test.

Step 2: Create a data sheet to use with each of your subjects. Leave a space at the top for the person's name, initial blood pressure, and initial heart rate, and create a column on the left with a row for each question. Along the top of the sheet, create the following headings: EYE CONTACT; FIDGETING; BLOOD PRESSURE; HEART RATE; OTHER NOTES; TRUTH/LIE. (If you're working alone, you can leave off the heading for heart rate.) If you have access to a copy machine, make a copy of this

form for each person you plan to test. Alternately, create the data sheet in a word-processing program and print out numerous copies.

Step 3: Choose who will be taking your test. It's better to work with people you don't know too well, so you won't have personal insight into their answers that will inform you as to whether they're lying or not. Teachers, friends of your parents, or siblings of your friends are good choices.

Step 4: One at a time, meet with your subjects in the room you've chosen for administering the test. Have the subject sit at the table and make himself comfortable. Place the cuff of the blood pressure monitor on the person's arm and record his initial blood pressure by carefully following the instructions that come with the monitor.

Explain to your subject that you're going to be asking ten questions and you want him to lie to you on at least four, but no more than six, of his answers. Ask him to make a mental note of which questions he answers with lies.

Step 5: If you are working with a partner, have her place the stethoscope on the subject's chest and find his heartbeat. Using the clock or stopwatch, get a reading of the subject's heart rate by counting the beats that happen in six seconds. Multiply this number by ten and you have the rate in beats per minute. For a slightly more accurate reading, count the heartbeats for ten seconds and multiply this number by six. Record this number on the top of the chart. Your partner will continue to listen to the heartbeat throughout the test, counting the beats per minute as the subject gives his answers, and marking these counts down on a piece of paper.

Step 6: Administer the test. One at a time, ask your subject each of the questions on your sheet. As he answers, observe his body movements and mark any relevant observations on your data sheet. Take a blood pressure reading while the person is answering or immediately following his answer. Your partner should find a heart rate in the middle or toward the end of the answer.

When you've finished asking all the questions, have your partner fill in her observations on the data sheet. Look over the data you collected and see if there are any telltale signs of lying when a particular answer was given. Increased heart rate and blood pressure are signs of lying, as are fidgety or irregular body movements. Decide on which questions you believe your subject was telling the truth and on which he lied, and indicate this on the data sheet. (It's important to note that things like fidgeting or avoiding eye contact aren't necessarily signs of lying in themselves—the best signs to look for are changes from a person's normal behavior. If a normally fidgety, unfocused person suddenly sits very still and maintains strong eye contact, that can be just as strong a sign.)

Step 7: Share your conclusions with your subject and find out how many times you were right. When

you've finished all your subjects, compare your results. Did you get better at detecting lies? Were there some behaviors all people shared when lying? Were some people (like Chancellor Palpatine) much better at lying than others? Now that you've heightened your senses for these observations, perhaps you'll be able to detect a lie even without the help of reading blood pressure or heart rate!

TRICKING YOUR EYES: OPTICAL ILLUSIONS

When Luke trains with Yoda on Dagobah, he meets with some frustration but also makes great progress. His connection with the Force grows constantly, and his confidence grows as well. But when Luke enters a mysterious cave, he is forced to confront his greatest fear: facing off against Darth Vader. Luke is undone by this experience despite the fact that what he saw in the cave was only a figment of his imagination. The human brain works in mysterious ways, and it's possible for all of us to see things that aren't there . . . or completely miss things that are. This activity will give you some experience with how our eyes and brains work together to show us what's there . . . and what's not!

WHAT YOU NEED:

TIME REQUIRED:
30 MINUTES

- **White paper**
- **Black marker**
- **Cardboard**
- **Compass or circular object about 4" across, like the lid of a large yogurt container**
- **Scissors**
- **Glue or rubber cement**
- **A spinning top**
- **Thick toothpick or cooking skewer**
- **Willing participants**

COST:
$ $ $

LEVEL:

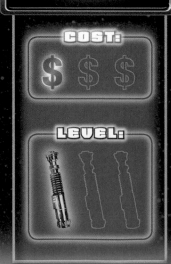

EXPERIMENT #1: In this part, you'll get your eye (and the eyes of others!) to see something that isn't there.

Step 1: Using either your compass or circular lid, draw a circle on the white paper. Next, copy a pattern (below) onto your circle. When you've finished, use the scissors to cut out the main shapes. Draw the same-sized circle on the cardboard and cut this circle out as well. Use the glue or rubber cement to adhere the patterned circle to the cardboard.

Step 2: Use the scissors to make a small hole in the center of the circle. If you're using a top or dreidel, push the paper onto the stem so the black markings face up. You might like to use a little glue or rubber cement to hold the paper in place on the top. If you're making your own top, push a toothpick or skewer through the middle of the disc so about ½ inch sticks out underneath. Break or cut away the top so you have a 1-inch stem.

Step 3: Practice spinning the top until you can get it to spin smoothly for as long as possible. Once you've gotten your spin down, spin the top and look at it from directly above. What do you see? Have other people try this as well. Show them the top, spin it for them or have them try spinning it themselves, and ask what appears to their eyes.

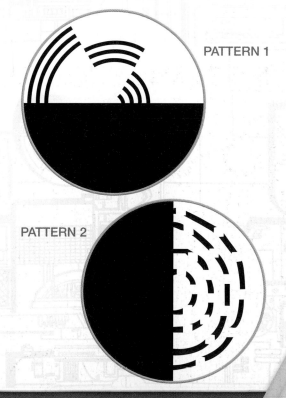

PATTERN 1

PATTERN 2

EXPERIMENT #2: This part works with blind spots. You should alternately be able to see things that AREN'T there and NOT see other things that ARE there.

Step 1: Copy or trace one of the images from the next page onto separate strips of white paper. Use your scissors to cut rectangles that are approximately ½ inch by 8 inches.

Your dot and plus sign should be about 6 inches apart.

Step 2: Start by holding one of the test strips at arm's length from your face, directly level with your eyes. Close one eye and focus your attention on the image on the opposite side of the paper (if you close your right eye, look at the object on the left side of the paper). Slowly bring the strip closer to your face. At a certain point, does what you see change? If you keep moving the paper closer to your face, does the image change again?

Try switching eyes and looking at the other side of the paper. Once you've tried everything with the first test strip, try one of the others. You will see different effects with each of the different strips.

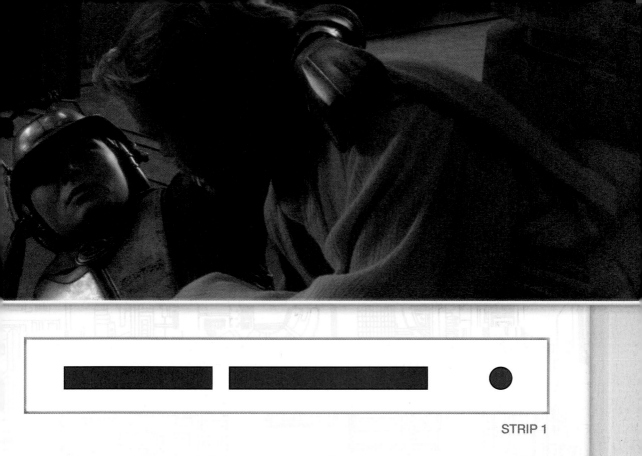

STRIP 1

STRIP 2

STRIP 3

THE Secret:

When our eyes aren't able to make sense of the information they receive, our brains fill in the rest. This can happen for different reasons. Take the case of Benham's disc, which was developed by a toy maker in 1894. We know we have different cells in the eye that affect vision in different ways. In the retina, located at the back of our eyeball, red, blue, and green are each perceived with different kinds of cells. All three kinds activate when we see white, but they activate at different speeds. When we send a lot of indecipherable information to the eye—as the spinning Benham's disc does—the rapid switching of black and white fools some of these vision cells into firing after the others have stopped, and our brains are forced to make sense of something while receiving confusing information.

In the case of blind spots, there is a spot in our retina where the optic nerve leaves the eye and goes to the brain. This nerve carries the visual information to the brain so we can decipher images. But where the nerve stem passes through the retina, it disrupts the cells used for vision, leaving a spot that doesn't react to light. Rather than have a spot in our vision with nothing in it, our brain fills in the spot with what seems to make sense given the context of the rest of what we're seeing—but sometimes what our brain puts there isn't actually reality!

GROW YOUR OWN CRYSTALS

The lightsaber is the weapon of choice for Jedi Knights and Sith warriors. These powerful blades of pure energy are unique and difficult to replace. Luke inherited his father's lightsaber, but lost it (and his hand!) in a battle with Darth Vader. After a long time and much effort, Luke pulled together the pieces he needed to construct a new lightsaber, but he could not find the crystal he needed to complete the weapon. Finally, Luke found instructions to grow his own crystal, with which he finished his new lightsaber. Here's a recipe for you to grow your own crystal so you won't have to work as long as Luke to put a lightsaber together.

WHAT YOU NEED:

- **Alum powder***
- **Teaspoon**
- **Hot water**
- **2 clean glass jars, 12 ounces or larger**
- **Fluorescent ink**
- **Coffee filter, napkin, cloth, or paper towel**
- **Pencil or other sticklike object**
- **Thread**

*Alum powder is often used in pickling and can be found in the spice section of many grocery stores.

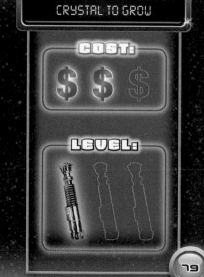

TIME REQUIRED:
20-MINUTE SET UP, 24 HOURS TO SIT, SEVERAL DAYS FOR CRYSTAL TO GROW

COST:
$ $ $

LEVEL:

WHAT TO DO:

Step 1: Fill your glass jar with hot water. Heat some water on the stove or in the microwave. The water needs to be hot but not boiling.

Step 2: If you're using fluorescent ink, add it now. Add about a teaspoon of liquid ink or squeeze the ink from one marker into the water while wearing gloves. Make sure the water is cool enough to be safe if you're going to touch it. If you need to reheat the water in a microwave after you've added the ink, that's fine.

Step 3: Add the alum powder one teaspoon at a time and stir until the powder dissolves completely. Continue adding powder until it will no longer dissolve and begins to collect at the bottom of the jar. Try to prevent too much powder from settling at the bottom by not adding too much at once.

Step 4: Cover the top of the jar with a coffee filter, cloth towel, paper towel, or napkin and allow the jar to sit undisturbed for 24 hours. When the time has passed, examine the jar. You should have some small crystals forming at the bottom. If you don't see any crystals, let the jar sit for another day and try again. If you still don't see any crystals, you may need to start over. Try making the water hotter when you start adding the alum; this will allow you to dissolve more powder into the solution.

Step 5: Once you've identified small crystals—called seeds—pour the solution into the second jar and collect the crystals on a piece of paper. Select the largest and best-formed crystal to act as the seed for your large crystal.

Step 6: Cut a piece of thread that will be a little longer than half of your jar and tie one end to your crystal seed. Tie the other end to the pencil or comparable object. Test to see if your seed will hang in the middle of the second jar by placing the pencil across the mouth so the crystal hangs down from it into the jar below. You may need to adjust the length of the string so the crystal isn't too close to the top or bottom of the jar.

If you're using fluorescent ink and a black light, find a dark room and shine the black light on your crystal. The results should be illuminating!

Step 7: Once you have the length of your string arranged, find a place for your solution to sit for several days (or even weeks), cover it with the coffee filter or towel, and leave it undisturbed. Periodically check to see how your crystal is doing. When it reaches a size you're happy with, remove it from the solution and allow it to dry on the papertowel. From now on, keep your crystal away from moisture, which can break down some of the crystal that has formed.

THE Secret:

Crystals form when molecules of a substance are dissolved in a solution and then begin to stick together and come out of that solution. As the molecules stick together, more molecules are attracted to them, and the crystal grows. Under these conditions, most substances form solids with a particular formation of molecules, and oftentimes this creates the form that we see as crystals. Environmental factors, such as how much material is dissolved, what speed the solution cools, or the rate of evaporation, can affect the size and success of crystal formation. To take this experiment further, think of ways you can change the crystal-forming environment. What if you place the jars in a cool place, like a refrigerator, or a warm place, like near a water heater? Does this change the crystals that form? What if you speed the rate of evaporation by placing the jar near a fan? What other variations can you think of?

MICROSCOPIC LIFE

I n the *Star Wars* universe, the Jedi are able to connect with the Force through "midi-chlorians," microscopic organisms that live in the cells of all living things. Qui-Gon tells Anakin that those who possess high quantities of midi-chlorians in their blood can understand the will of the Force itself. In order to see organisms as small as midi-chlorians, you'd probably need a very powerful (and expensive!) microscope. But with a more accessible microscope, you can get a detailed look at the microscopic single-celled life that surrounds us in the real world.

WHAT YOU NEED:

- **Large jar, plastic container, or small aquarium**
- **Dead grass or leaf matter**
- **1–2 cups of water**
- **Dropper**
- **Depression slide, or flat slide and cover slip***
- **Notebook and pencil**
- **Microscope with changeable objective lenses, magnification of at least 400x****
- **Internet access**

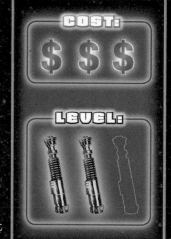

TIME REQUIRED:
1 WEEK FOR SOAKING, AS MUCH TIME AS YOU LIKE FOR OBSERVATIONS

COST:
$ $ $

LEVEL:

*Depression slides are a single piece of glass or plastic with a small depression where your drop of water can rest while you observe it under the microscope. Wet mounts are made with a flat slide and a coverslip which creates a single thin layer of water to observe. You will need to scan through the different depths of the drop to make all of your observations.

**It's possible to purchase supplies through an online scientific supplier for use at your home, but we recommend asking your science teacher to let you use the microscope and slides at school.

Step 1: Fill a large jar, plastic container, or aquarium with water and let it sit open overnight. (Our drinking water is chlorinated, and allowing the water to sit overnight will let the chlorine evaporate out of the water. Otherwise it may kill anything living when you add your grass or leaves.)

Step 2: Collect some dead grass or leaf matter from somewhere near your school or home. One or two cups of material will be plenty. Submerge this in the water that has sat out overnight, and make sure it's all wet. If you have to pour out some water to make room for your leaves, that's ok. Just make sure you have enough water so that it won't all be absorbed by the material you add. Find somewhere your container can sit for a week without being disturbed. The spot shouldn't be too hot (in direct sunlight) or too cold.

Step 3: If you're working at home, bring your container, dropper, and slide materials to a work surface where you can set up your microscope. If you're bringing your material to school to work with a microscope there, cover your water and cutting mixture and bring it to school. You can simply take some of the mixture out and put it in a smaller jar if you prefer. Ask your science teacher where you can work, and set up your microscope with your slide materials, dropper, and cutting mixture nearby.

Step 4: To make the first slide, use your dropper to suck up some water from near the grass or leaves. With the slide on the table, put 1 to 3 drops onto it. If you're using a depression slide, put the water in the depression, and carefully place it on the microscope stage without spilling the drop. If you're making a

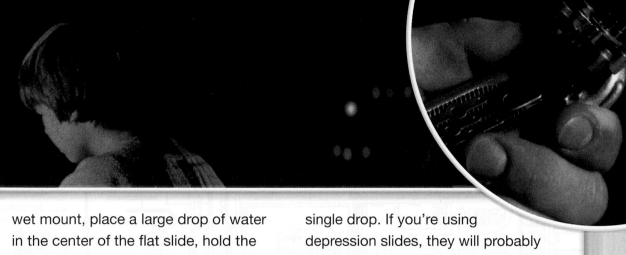

wet mount, place a large drop of water in the center of the flat slide, hold the cover slip at a 45-degree angle, and bring the bottom edge into contact with the water so the rest of the cover slip is hanging over the drop. Gently let the slide drop. You should see the water spread out evenly between the cover slip and the slide. It may not fill the entire square of the cover slip, which is fine.

Step 5: Place your slide on the stage of the microscope and position it so the water is centered over the stage opening. Set the microscope to its lowest magnification and bring the stage to its highest setting (closest to the lens). Looking into the microscope, slowly lower the stage until you see something. You may need to scan up and down a few times before you find anything. Scan slowly and always return to the top to begin your scan. Once you find something, use the fine adjustment to bring your view into sharp focus. You should be able to find numerous small organisms in a

single drop. If you're using depression slides, they will probably be swimming around and harder to focus on. On a wet mount, once you focus on one organism, it may be easier to move the slide around as you look for others, which will likely be around the same depth. If you're having trouble finding anything, ask an adult to help you look. Sometimes it can be helpful to include a small bit of grass or leaf on the slide, because the organisms are usually close to these objects to begin with.

Keep track of what you find in your notebook. Describe or sketch the different organisms you discover and make notes about the relative abundance of each kind. If you want, you can use the Internet to try and identify some of the critters you discover. (You could use specific search terms like "microscopic aquatic bacteria in leafy soil," and so on.)

THE Secret:

We may not have midi-chlorians here on Earth, but we do have a mind-boggling variety of microscopic life living all around us all the time. They live on our furniture, our food, our skin — and even our eyelashes!

What do you think the role of these organisms is in nature? Do you think they're important? Believe it or not, despite the fact that we can't see them with our bare eyes, our world wouldn't be the same without them. Many of these organisms are an important part of breaking down dead organic matter so that nutrients can be returned to the earth and reused by living plants. Sure, some of these organisms are harmful and can make us sick (whatever you do, don't drink the water from your sample!), but the majority of them are harmless to us. Many are even critical to the ecosystem. Who knew so much was happening all around us all the time?

TEST YOUR REFLEXES

O nce, before the execution of Order 66 by Chancellor Palpatine, there were many Jedi throughout the galaxy. Younglings trained at the Jedi Temple on Coruscant, where they learned to connect to the Force and practiced dueling with lightsabers to perfect their reflexes. Are the lightning-quick reflexes of the Jedi unique to these warriors, or could others have similarly fast responses? Here's an experiment that will help you determine who among your friends and family has the sharpest reflexes . . . maybe you'll find a few potential Jedi hidden in your midst!

WHAT YOU NEED:

- **Yardstick**
- **Construction paper or cardboard**
- **Scissors**
- **Markers**
- **Glue or tape**
- **Notebook and pencil**
- **Willing test subjects**

TIME REQUIRED:
10 TO 15 MINUTES TO
SET UP, MOMENTS TO
RUN EACH TEST

COST:

$ $ $

LEVEL:

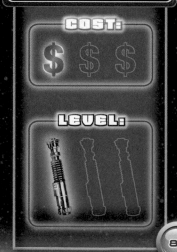

Step 1: Due to the constant force of gravity, objects fall at a fairly constant rate (wind resistance notwithstanding). Scientists have calculated the rate at which an object (like a yardstick) approaches the ground as it falls, which allows us to determine the distance by matching it with the length of time that has passed. Determining this rate is the hardest part of this experiment—but it's been done for you!

Step 2: Copy the following distances and times in your notebook:

Distance	Time
2 in.	0.10 sec.
4 in.	0.14 sec.
6 in.	0.17 sec.
8 in.	0.20 sec.
10 in.	0.23 sec.
12 in.	0.25 sec.
17 in.	0.30 sec.
24 in.	0.35 sec.
31 in.	0.40 sec.

Step 3: To give people the test, you hold the yardstick from above. Have your subject hold an open hand around the very bottom of the yardstick at the inch marked ZERO. Explain that they should try to catch the yardstick as quickly as possible when they realize you've dropped it. Without telling them, release the yardstick and let it fall. When they've caught it, record in your notebook how far the yardstick fell in the time that elapsed and what reaction time this corresponds to. Let each person try at least three times and see if their reaction improves. Don't forget to test yourself! To do so you'll need to have someone else drop the yardstick for you. It's impossible for you to drop with one hand without the other hand knowing what's coming!

Step 4: If you're able to test a lot of people, you'll have an opportunity to draw some conclusions from your data. Were some people faster than others? Were there trends in who was faster and who was slower? How did older people's reactions compare with younger people's? What about girls and boys? Did athletes seem to react more quickly? If you were going to select students for Jedi training, are there particular people you'd like to work with?

PART III
REPUBLIC KNOW-HOW

TESTING RUST ON DIFFERENT METALS

Our favorite heroes would frequently be lost or caught in a tight bind without their two indispensible friends — droids R2-D2 and C-3PO. They appear alongside Padmé and Anakin, and later assist Luke and Leia. How do machines that go through as much as these two (space battles, sandstorms, swamp exploration, forest treks, and so on) last so many years? In this experiment, you'll test different metals to see if some are more resistant to rust and corrosion than others. Then you'll have an idea of where to start if you ever design your own durable droid companion.

WHAT YOU NEED:

TIME REQUIRED:
15 MINUTES TO SET UP,
UP TO A WEEK OR MORE TO
MAKE OBSERVATIONS

- **Solid metal wire* made of different metals but the same diameter, such as:**
  - copper
  - aluminum
  - zinc
  - nickel chromium
  - steel or iron
  - stainless steel
  - zinc-coated steel
- **Water**

- **Salt**
- **Tablespoon**
- **Pencil and paper**
- **Scissors**
- **Tape**
- **3 large jars or glasses**
- **3 pencils for each type of metal you test**

COST:

$ $ $

LEVEL:

*Metal wires can be purchased online or at your local hardware store.
Do NOT use enameled wire, because the enamel will affect your results.

WHAT TO DO:

Step 1: Choose which metals you will be testing and cut three 5-inch strips of each type. Make sure to keep track of which metal is which.

Step 2: Loosely wrap each strip of wire around the bottom third of a pencil so there is about a ¼ to ½ inch of space between each coil. For each metal, make small labels with your paper and pencil. Use the tape to attach the labels to the top of the appropriate pencils. You should have three wire-wrapped pencils per metal and labels for each type of metal you are testing.

Step 3: Fill one jar with about 5 inches of water so that when you place a pencil in the jar in the next step, the wire will be submerged but your labels will stay dry. Fill the second jar with 5 inches of water as well, and then dissolve a tablespoon of salt in the water. It's fine if some of the salt settles to the bottom. Leave the third jar empty.

Step 4: Place one pencil of each metal in each of your jars. Make sure the pencils are spaced so the metals aren't touching each other, and that the wires are submerged completely. When you're finished, you should have one wire coil of each metal in freshwater, saltwater, and the empty jar.

Step 5: For the next week or two, check your wires daily and make observations. Record these observations in your notebook. You can make a table (see below) with a row for each type of metal and a column for each date, divided into three sections for notes on the freshwater, saltwater, and the empty jar.

At the end of the observation period, summarize your observations. Is one metal clearly more resistant to rust than the others? Does the environment the metal is in make a difference? If you had to build a droid that was made to last, which type of metal would you use?

DAY 1	Freshwater	Saltwater	Empty jar
Copper			
Aluminum			
Zinc			
Nickel chromium			
Steel			
Iron			
Stainless steel			
Zinc-coated steel			

PROTECTIVE COATINGS AND METALS

The *Star Wars* universe is full of vehicles, droids, and weapons that are built with strong metals to withstand the test of time. R2-D2 and C-3PO survive harsh climates and blaster bolts. Spaceships, like the *Millennium Falcon*, endure galactic battles and years of wear and tear. Weapons such as lightsabers are used for decades. In addition to the choice of metal, what else can ensure the long life of our friendly droids, important ships, and tools? In this activity, you'll discover how the addition of a protective coating can guard metal from rust and corrosion.

WHAT YOU NEED:

- **3 large glass or plastic containers**

- **6 or more small pieces, approx. 1" or 2" square, of each metal you decide to test*** such as:
  - steel or iron
  - aluminum
  - stainless steel
  - copper

- **Metal shears or strong scissors**

- **Water**

- **Salt**

- **Tablespoon**

- **Large jar or container**

- **Metal coatings*** such as:
  - Clear nail polish
  - Spray-on car wax
  - Primer for metals
  - Vegetable oil
  - Furniture varnish

- **Brushes or rags**

- **Masking tape**

- **Marker**

TIME REQUIRED:
30 TO 60 MINUTES TO SET UP,
TWO WEEKS FOR
OBSERVATIONS

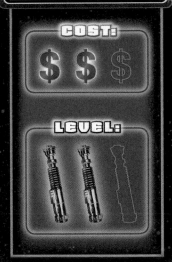

COST:

$ $ $

LEVEL:

*Sheet metal, varnish, and metal primers can be purchased online or at hardware stores.

(Note: It's only necessary to test one type of metal, but you can expand the experiment and compare different metals and their resistance to rusting if you use more than one. If you only use one, we recommend steel or iron, NOT stainless steel, which is formulated to prevent rusting and may not give you good results. Other metals may exhibit corrosion, but only those containing iron will form rust.)

Step 1: Select your metals for testing and prepare small squares of each type. You will want one square that will not be submerged in water, one for freshwater, one for saltwater, and one for each type of coating you want to test. Remember you only need to use one metal to answer the question about whether coatings can prevent rust or not, but if you do use

more than one, be sure to keep your metals separate so you know which is which.

Step 2: Choose which substances you will be using to coat your metal squares. You can use one or you can test the efficacy of different substances.

Apply a layer of coating, nail polish for example, to one side of the square and allow it to dry for 10 or 20 minutes. When that side is dry, flip the square and coat the other side. Be sure you coat the edges of the square as well. (If you're using vegetable oil or a similar coating, it will not dry, so simply wait to coat the object until just before you place it in the experimental setup.)

Step 3: In a large bottle or container, mix several tablespoons of salt with water. Use 2 to 3 tablespoons per liter. You will want about 3 cups (about ¾ of a liter) of saltwater for each metal you are testing. A 2-liter bottle should cover three or four tests.

Step 4: For each metal you are testing, set up six cups or containers. Fill two with 3 or 4 inches of fresh-water, two with 3 or 4 inches of salt-water, and leave two empty. Use the masking tape and marker to label the containers with the solution and the metal that will be in each. Find a place to set your containers where they can sit undisturbed for two weeks.

Step 5: For each metal, place a clean square into a freshwater, saltwater, and empty container. Next, place a coated square into the other freshwater, saltwater, and empty

container. Let the metals sit in the solutions for the next two weeks. Periodically, check your metals for any changes. Make notes of your observations in a table in your notebook. If you used more than one type of metal, consider the following questions: Which causes rust or corrosion to happen faster: saltwater or freshwater? Do different metals react differently to rust or corrosion, and is one less likely to suffer damage from a moist environment? Does coating metal prevent it from rusting or corroding, and do some coatings work better than others?

CLEANING METAL part 1

Despite one's best efforts, sometimes conditions lead to the rusting of a droid or spaceship. After R2-D2 repairs the Queen's ship in a daring escape from the Trade Federation, Padmé spends time cleaning the brave little droid — not just as a reward for his efforts, but to keep him clean and rust free. There are plenty of products on the market for cleaning rust and debris off metal, but is there a simpler solution right in your own home?

WHAT YOU NEED:

- **Rusted metal objects such as nails, tools, iron fencing, or a car surface***

- **Salt**

- **Lime or lemon**

- **White vinegar**

- **Aluminum foil**

- **Cola**

- **Cup or bowl**

- **Sink or clean rags or paper towels**

- **Commercial rust remover like naval jelly or others****

*Your metal objects can be different, but the more similar they are, the easier your comparisons will be. You will want one piece of metal (or section of metal on a large object like a car or fence) for each rust removal method you test.

**You can purchase commercial rust removers at your local hardware store.

WARNING: Be very careful when handling sharp and rusted items!

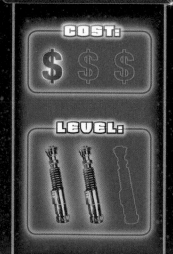

TIME REQUIRED:
30 TO 60 MINUTES,
PLUS TIME TO SIT FOR SOME
CLEANING SOLUTIONS

COST:
$ $ $

LEVEL:

WHAT TO DO:

Step 1: Collect your rusty objects and the substances you plan to test as cleaners. The following are used together: (1) salt and lemon or lime; (2) aluminum foil and vinegar; (3) aluminum foil and cola. Feel free to look up other home treatments for rust and test them out as well! If you have a camera, you might want to take "before" pictures that you can compare with photos taken after you clean each object.

Step 2: If you are using the salt and lemon or lime combination, set this one up first. Shake the salt over the object so it lightly coats the surface, and then squeeze the lemon or lime until the object is thoroughly wet. Let the solution sit on the rust for 2 to 3 hours, and then rub the surface with the rind of the lemon or lime.

Step 3: While your citrus-and-salt setup is sitting, pour about half a cup of vinegar into a cup or bowl. Dip a small piece of aluminum foil into the vinegar and then rub your second rusty item with the foil to remove the rust. Try both sides of the foil, because they may react differently. After rubbing for a while, rinse the object with water or wipe it with a dry paper towel or cloth to remove any residue.

Step 4: For your third rusty object, pour cola liberally over the rust. Let it sit for about 5 minutes, and then rub at the rust with a small square of aluminum foil. Once again, try using both sides of the foil to see if one side works better than the other. You can rinse the object or wipe it with a clean cloth to see your final results.

Step 5: Using your commercial rust remover, follow the instructions to treat your fourth rusty object. This will probably involve rags for applying the remover and wiping away the rust.

Step 6: Compare the results of your different methods. If you're using a camera, you can put "before" and "after" pictures of each object as evidence of how effective the cleaners were. Otherwise, make notes in your notebook about how effective each cleaner was. Did the rust come off? Was it easy to do? How much time and effort was needed for each technique to work? If you were faced with a rusty droid, which method would you use to get it cleaned up?

CLEANING METAL part 2

WHAT YOU NEED:

- **A large glass or plastic (not metal) container like an aquarium or trash can**

- **Flat sheet of iron or steel***

- **Washing soda****

- **Tablespoon**

- **Water**

- **Large spoon or stick**

- **Rubber gloves**

- **Work sink with soapy water and a scrubber**

- **3M finishing pads*****

- **2-amp or greater battery charger with positive and negative leads and clips******

- **A rusty tool or object*******

- **Duct tape**

> TIME REQUIRED:
> 30 MINUTES TO SET UP, 2 TO 5 HOURS TO RUN, 15 MINUTES FOR FINAL CLEANING AND OBSERVATION

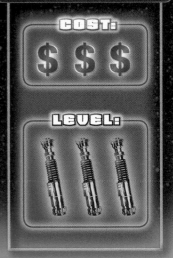

COST:

$ $ $

LEVEL:

*You can purchase sheet metal online or at the hardware store, but you can also use an inexpensive stainless steel pot top, baking sheet, or pan. The metal will corrode during the experiment so just make sure you're not borrowing a pot top from someone who expects to get it back!

**Washing soda can be found in the laundry detergent section of most grocery stores.

***The 3M finishing pad is a specially designed scouring pad. You can use other types of scouring pads, but the 3M model seems to work best without affecting the metal below the rust once you've cleared the damaged material away. They can be purchased inexpensively online or at hardware stores.

****Battery chargers can be purchased online or at home goods suppliers for less than $50.

*****The more rust your object has on it, the more dramatic this process will be. We recommend searching a work shed for an old tool that doesn't have too many nooks and crannies but has plenty of surface area. An old rusted hammer or hinge would work well.

WHAT TO DO:

Step 1: Find something rusty that you can clean, and a place to work. This process works well for any kind of tool or pieces of metal, but the more little crevices where rust can get, the more difficult it will be to clean it off. A simple, flat surface is ideal. Or, if you want to try to clean more intricately shaped tools, add a small wire brush to your list of materials and use this to help clean off the debris at the end. Before you begin, use the soapy water in your work sink and a scrubber to wash any oil, dirt, or other debris off the surface of the object. It must be totally clean for the procedure to work. You will produce hydrogen gas in this experiment, which is nontoxic but should be well ventilated and *never* produced near an open flame. We recommend doing this experiment outside or in an open garage or work space. Never cover the container while the experiment is running, so the gas can escape and disperse.

Step 2: Make sure the object you're cleaning can easily fit inside your large container with room to spare. Make adjustments to either the tool or the container if this isn't the case. You can use any container that isn't made of metal, but a clear glass or plastic tank will allow you to observe the reaction. Fill the container with water until it is deep enough to cover your object. Wearing your rubber gloves, add 1 tablespoon of washing soda for each gallon of water you use and stir the solution until the washing soda is dissolved. The washing soda isn't dangerous, but it can dry your skin if you touch it (so it's best to wear the gloves when you work with it or the solution containing it).

Step 3: Make sure the power on your battery charger is turned off. Connect the positive lead (the red side) of the battery charger to your sheet of steel. If you're using a pot lid, connect

it to one edge. You will want to keep the clip out of the water, so either keep the water shallow enough that the pot lid sticks out, or hang the lid into the water by securing the lead from the battery to the top of your tank with duct tape. It's not dangerous for the clip to get wet, but the reaction may corrode the clip if it's in the water.

Step 4: Connect the negative lead (the black side) of the battery charger to the object you are cleaning. Make sure the connection is secure and place the object in the tank so it is fully submerged in the washing soda solution. It's fine for the clip on the negative lead to be in the solution. Position the object you are cleaning so most of its surface area faces the metal connected to the positive side of your battery charger. Make sure the object you're cleaning and the metal sheet are not touching. You want 2 to 5 inches of space between them. If the object is rusty on multiple sides (or it

has several different faces), you may want to turn it so each side faces the metal sheet for at least an hour or two. *(Make sure to turn off the charger before turning the object.)* Or, if you're simply demonstrating the effect of the electrolysis, use an object with two clear sides and only expose one to the steel sheet. When you're finished, you'll have a "before" and "after" demo all in your one object!

Step 5: When your setup is complete, make sure no one is touching the water, and turn on the battery charger. If the charger has settings, set it to the highest current. *Never touch the water or the metal objects while the power is on.* You won't seriously hurt yourself, but you can get a nasty shock. Always turn off the battery charger before you touch the water, remove anything to check the progress of the cleaning, or reposition the object.

Soon after turning on the power, you should see bubbles start to form on the object you are cleaning. This means the process is working!

Step 6: Let the setup be for at least 2 hours. If you're trying to clean multiple sides of a tool, every 1 to 2 hours, turn off the power, put on your gloves, and turn the object so a new side faces the positive lead of your setup. When a side is finished cleaning, it should be dark gray or black in color. If this isn't the case, let it run until the color has changed.

Step 7: When all the sides you are cleaning have turned a dark gray or black, turn off the battery, remove the object from the water, and disconnect it from the battery. Using the soapy water in your work sink and a 3M pad (you can cut them in half and use a half at a time), wash away all black material until the metal below is revealed. If not all of the rust has been removed, reconnect the negative end of the battery charger to the object and place it back in the water. Turn on the battery charger and allow the experiment to run until a new layer of dark residue has appeared. Repeat this step until the metal you are cleaning is rust free.

You can use this technique to clean any and all rusty objects at home. Just remember that once you're finished, the metal will start to rust again. If you want to keep it rust free, you will need to treat it with a protective seal or wax coating.

THE Secret:

The process of electrolysis causes electrons (negatively charged particles) to move from one metal object, through water, and into another metal object. The washing soda provides a solution that facilitates the movement of the electrons. The battery charger sends electrons into the object you're cleaning, which travel toward the positively charged metal in the water, reacting with the water as they go. This causes hydrogen gas bubbles to form, which forcibly loosen any rust or debris from the surface of the metal. At the same time, the reaction that caused the rust to form, the oxidation of the metal, is reversed, and the rust is changed back into a form of metal. This is why the color changes from orange to gray or black. This metal is porous and not tightly adhered to the surface of the object, so it can be removed when you scrub the metal with a finishing pad.

TRAINING WORMS

Repeated attempts are made on Senator Amidala's life. Her enemies go so far as to use poisonous millipede-like creatures against her. While the Senator sleeps, two deadly kouhuns are released into her chamber — a single bite from either of them will be enough to do the job. Fortunately, Anakin arrives just in time to destroy the venomous creatures. But would it really be possible to train such simple animals to do such a specific job?

WHAT YOU NEED:

TIME REQUIRED: 10 TO 15 MINUTES TO SET UP, MOMENTS TO RUN EACH TEST

- Shallow plastic storage bin or box, approximately 2' x 2' x 6"
- Extra cardboard
- Aluminum foil or plastic wrap
- Scissors
- Glue and/or tape
- Soil
- Coffee can or other container with a lid that can be punctured

- Water
- Pen or hammer and nail or screwdriver
- Spray bottle
- Fruit slices, not citrus; apples or bananas work
- Stopwatch or clock
- Red lightbulb
- A dark room
- Worm*
- Notebook and pencil

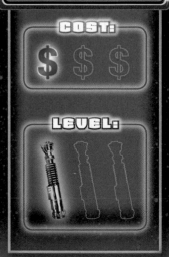

COST:
$ $ $

LEVEL:

*Remember, even if you don't like them, worms are living creatures. Treat them with care and release them when you're finished with your experiment.

We don't want you to work with anything poisonous, but with just an earthworm and a maze, you'll discover whether invertebrates can accomplish complex tasks.

Step 1: Go find a worm! (This is fun, because you never know what else you may come across in the process.) Find somewhere outdoors where there are rocks and tree trunks or large branches on the ground. Carefully lift the rocks or wood and move it to one side and see if there are any worms underneath. You want as large a worm as possible, so don't settle for the first small one you find. Keep looking until you find a big night crawler. When you find your subject, put a few inches of dirt in your coffee can or other container and set your worm inside. If the sides are tall enough, you may be able to leave the container open. You can also place a lid on top, but be sure to put several small air holes in it. You can use a pen, a hammer and nail, or a screwdriver to do this. If the soil you're using isn't damp, take out the worm and spray the soil with just enough water to dampen it. Don't spray the worm directly. Give the worm a piece of fruit and leave it alone for about a day. Be sure to check the moisture in the worm's container once in a while so the worm doesn't get too dry, which will kill it.

Step 2: Build your maze. The shallow box will be the base of your maze, and you will make walls using the extra cardboard. If you're using a cardboard box as your base, first create your walls. Use the scissors to cut the cardboard into strips with

6-inch sides to create your maze. You don't want the maze to be too difficult, so figure on making three or four turns to get to the end, and two or three wrong turns available on the way. Use the glue to position the walls and allow them to set before continuing. Once the glue is dry, cover all the cardboard surfaces inside the maze with tinfoil or plastic wrap and use the glue or tape to seal the seams. If you're using a plastic base, before gluing the walls in place, cover them with aluminum foil or plastic wrap. You will be adding water to the maze and you want to protect the cardboard from getting wet. When the walls are in place and all the cardboard surfaces are waterproofed, add a thin layer of soil—half an inch is plenty—to the bottom of the maze. This will give the worm a surface to move on, but you

don't want it deep enough for the worm to bury itself.

Step 3: At least 12 hours before you're ready to test your worm in the maze, remove the fruit from its container. A little longer is better, but don't leave the worm without food for more than a full day.

Step 4: Check the moisture in your maze soil. If it's dry, use the spray bottle to dampen it. You don't want the soil to be wet, just damp. Move into a room you can darken and replace one lightbulb in the room with the red lightbulb. Worms are nocturnal and aren't likely to be active in bright light. By using the red light, you create the sense of nighttime, but in a way that allows you to watch the worm. Turn off all the lights but the red light. Put a piece of fruit at the end of the maze, place the worm at your starting point, and start the clock! Watch the worm and see how long it takes to find the piece of fruit. The first trial may take a while, so you might want to have something else to keep you busy while you wait. When the worm has reached the fruit, make a record of the time in your notebook. Create a table for the date and time of each trial.

Step 5: Place the worm back in its container with another piece of fruit overnight. In the morning, remove the fruit and prepare the worm for another trial. Repeat Steps 3 and 4 for one or two weeks and see if the worm gets better at solving the maze. If the times get consistently shorter, then the worm is figuring it out!

Note: It's possible to try this test with other, faster-moving creatures like beetles, cockroaches, or millipedes. The problem with these animals is that they can climb the walls of the maze. If you want to try an insect with legs, place a piece of plastic wrap over the top of the maze and glue it to the tops of the walls and maze edges so the insect has to follow the maze and can't take shortcuts. Leave only a small corner unglued at the start and at the finish of the maze so you can put the insect in and out, and refresh the fruit and use tape to seal those places while you run the trial.

FIRE SAFETY
part 1

After Han Solo narrowly escapes the Death Star in his *Millennium Falcon*, an electrical fire ignited that — left unchecked — could have done major damage. Fortunately, R2-D2 used his own fire extinguisher to get things under control and save the ship. Whatever it was R2 sprayed on the flames, we know for sure it wasn't water. Pouring water on an electrical fire is one of the most dangerous things you can do. But what other way is there to put out a flame? As it turns out, there are safer and cleaner ways to stop a fire from getting out of hand. Try these two activities to see that water isn't the only substance that stops a fire in its tracks.

WHAT YOU NEED:

**TIME REQUIRED:
30 MINUTES**

- Candle (a birthday or tea-light candle will work)

- Clay or rubber cement

- Matches or a lighter*

- Baking soda

- Tablespoon

- White vinegar

- A plastic container that is taller than your candle and wide enough to allow the candle to be lit; a coffee can or similar-shaped container works well

COST:

$ $ $

LEVEL:

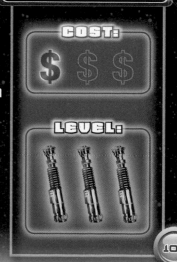

*Always have an adult help you when using matches or a lighter.

Step 1: Use the clay or glue to stand your candle in the bottom of your container. If you're using a tea light, you can simply place it in the container.

Step 2: Use the measuring spoon to place 3 tablespoons of baking soda in the bottom of the container surrounding the candle. Be careful not to get baking soda on the candle.

Step 3: Have an adult help you carefully light the candle.

Step 4: Use the measuring spoon again to measure 2 tablespoons of vinegar. Pour the vinegar carefully into the container so it runs down the sides and doesn't splash the candle. If necessary, you can gently tip the container to combine the baking soda and vinegar. Once the two are reacting, watch what happens to the candle. If nothing happens, repeat Steps 2 and 3 with slightly more baking soda and vinegar.

FIRE SAFETY
part 2

The heroes of Star Wars always seem to be putting out fires — whether literally or figuratively. It often comes down to the faithful droid R2-D2 to do the grunt work, though. Being such a capable droid, he has more than one way to put out a fire. In this experiment, you'll learn a second way to put out a fire with the same substances as Part 1.

WHAT YOU NEED:

- **Same candle from Part 1 or a regular taper candle and candlestick**

- **Matches or a lighter***

- **1- or 2-liter bottle**

- **Tablespoon**

- **3 tablespoons of baking soda**

- **2 tablespoons of vinegar**

**TIME REQUIRED:
30 MINUTES**

COST:

$ $ $

LEVEL:

*Always have an adult help you when using matches or a lighter.

WHAT TO DO:

Step 1: Set up a single taper candle, like the candle from Part 1. Set this on a clean work space with no papers or debris nearby, and carefully light the candle.

Step 2: In the plastic bottle, combine 3 tablespoons of baking soda with 2 tablespoons of vinegar. Swirl the substances around so they are reacting.

Step 3: Holding the opening of the bottle a few inches above the candle, turn the bottle on its side. Be careful not to spill any of the baking soda and vinegar mixture. Hold the bottle steadily over the candle and watch what happens.

THE Secret:

Fire needs several things to burn, but without oxygen a flame won't survive. The reaction of baking soda and vinegar creates carbon dioxide gas, which fire can't consume. When the gas fills the container around the candle, or falls around the candle from the bottle (carbon dioxide is heavier than our atmosphere), it pushes the oxygen away from the candle, which stops it from being able to burn. Carbon dioxide fire extinguishers work the same way but with much greater quantities of carbon dioxide gas in order to put out larger fires. They're an important tool in putting out electrical fires, which can be made worse if you pour water on them. Remember, if your spaceship is on fire, reach for the CO_2, not the H_2O!

HOMEMADE PERISCOPE

When Luke Skywalker crashes into a murky swamp on Dagobah, R2 gets out of his astromech socket to assess the situation. When something rocks the ship, he winds up in the swamp, which is deeper than it looks. Luke worries that R2 may be lost for good, but a few seconds later, the plucky droid deploys his periscope — a tool used to get a view of a place otherwise blocked from view — and finds his way to shore. Here's a plan to use the reflective power of mirrors to make your own periscope.

WHAT YOU NEED:

- **2 identical small mirrors***
- **Long cardboard or plywood, or 4' to 6' of PVC piping****
- **Scissors or saw*****
- **Wood glue**
- **Duct tape**
- **Ruler**

*We recommend rectangular mirrors from the health and beauty section of online suppliers or drug stores. Small rectangular locker mirrors are also a good choice.

**Your periscope will work with inexpensive materials such as cardboard, plywood, or even multiple milk cartons (created by cutting off the bottoms and tops and connecting them with duct tape). Another option is to create a periscope using PVC piping. This will be more durable but is more expensive. It will also require having the pipe cut, or purchasing 90-degree connectors to allow for viewing of the mirrors.

***Always have an adult help you with dangerous tools like saws. You only need a saw if you're building with plywood.

TIME REQUIRED:
30 TO 60 MINUTES
DEPENDING ON MATERIALS

COST:
$ $ $

LEVEL:

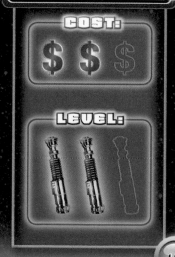

Step 1: Find your mirrors. It's important to have your mirrors in place first, so you know what dimensions the body of your periscope should have. Use the ruler to measure the length of the sides of your mirrors, or the diameter if you're using round mirrors.

Step 2: Choose what type of material you will use to build your periscope and have it ready. Cardboard is the easiest to come by and assemble, but will be relatively fragile. Plywood is a good, sturdy material, but will require more time to prepare and build. If you decide to use PVC piping, you will want to use round mirrors that are slightly smaller in diameter than your pipe.

Step 3: Build a long rectangular tube from your material with the same dimensions as your mirror. If you are using round mirrors, cut a piece of wood or cardboard that is slightly larger than your mirrors and mount them on this using the glue. Measure the sides of the mounted mirror and use these dimensions for the body of your periscope. The mirrors should be slightly smaller than the body, so they can be positioned inside. Your periscope can be any length you like, but we recommend a length of 4 to 6 feet. At the very top of the periscope, cut a rectangular opening that's slightly larger than the mirrors out of one side. Cut another out of the opposite side, at the very bottom. Use small rectangles of your material to cover the top and bottom openings of the periscope, so the rectangular windows are the only openings into the tube. Use the glue to secure the sides of the periscope body. You may need to do these one at a time and allow them to dry before moving to the next side. You can reinforce the corners with duct tape if you like.

Step 4: Place the mirrors inside the body of the periscope where you've made the rectangular viewing openings. The mirrors should be slanted at a 45-degree angle and should be parallel to each other. When you look into a rectangular opening, you should be looking at the slanted mirror. Use the glue to attach one edge of the mirror to the short side of the periscope close to the rectangular opening, and the other end of the mirror to the long side of the scope opposite the opening. See the diagram for clarity. Position the second mirror in the same way at the other end of the scope. Let the glue dry.

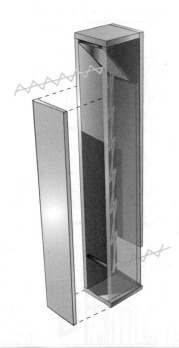

Step 5: You're ready to go viewing! Put one end of the periscope above a wall or hold it horizontally so one end passes a corner. Then, look through the opposite end. The mirrors will reflect light from one end to the other so you can see high up, down low, or around corners.

Note: It's possible to make a periscope for viewing underwater from above, but you need to change three things. First, choose materials that are waterproof, like plastic. You could use milk cartons or 2-liter bottles with the ends cut off and covered with aluminum foil for this version. Second, instead of two rectangular viewing windows, make one and leave one end of the scope open. Cover this end with clear plastic or glass held in place with the glue. Third, you only need one mirror positioned as before with the rectangular window. The other end will not have a mirror. Put the covered end into the water and look through the window at the top. Now you should have a special view into the depths below!

STUDYING LASERS

Blasters are fired in battles throughout the galaxy. Beams of particle energy and light shoot out of the weapons with devastating effects on their targets. But beams don't always stop when they hit a surface. When Luke, Leia, Han, and Chewbacca are trapped in a trash compactor, a blaster is fired and the beam bounces dangerously around the metal compartment. Have you ever wondered about the nature of lasers and how they move? You can't test a blaster, but observing a laserbeam can give you an idea of how these blasters work, and when it might be a good idea to hold your fire.

WHAT YOU NEED:

TIME REQUIRED:
20 MINUTES TO MAKE GELATIN, SEVERAL HOURS FOR GELATIN TO SET, 30 MINUTES FOR TESTS AND OBSERVATIONS

- **1 package each of gelatin dessert: red, blue, and green**
- **Measuring cup**
- **Water**
- **3 round, clear glass containers with flat bottoms, approximately 5 inches in diameter**
- **Refrigerator**
- **Red laser pointer***
- **Bowl or sink larger than the three containers, and hot water**
- **White plate**
- **White paper**
- **Knife**
- **Flashlight with adjustable-focus beam****
- **Spatula**

COST:
$ $ $

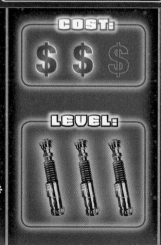
LEVEL:

*Red laser pointers can be purchased inexpensively online.

**Flashlights with beams you can focus can be purchased online for around $15. This part of the experiment is optional.

WARNING: Preparing gelatin desserts requires boiling water. Be sure to have an adult help you if you are using a stove, and take caution when working with the hot water.

WHAT TO DO:

Step 1: Make the three different colors of gelatin by following the instructions on the packages. You want to use the three different colors because of the way they each interact with the red laser beam. We see color as a result of pigments absorbing different wavelengths of light. The wavelengths that aren't absorbed are the ones that reflect and enter our eyes as a certain color. You will see something different in each color gelatin when you shine the red laser into them. Pour each gelatin mixture into its own flat-bottomed container and place them in a refrigerator for several hours until they are completely set.

Step 2: When the desserts are set, remove them from the refrigerator and place them on a clean work space. Have your white plate, knife, and spatula nearby. One at a time, shine the laser into the side of each of the gelatins so the beam is parallel with the table and the top of the dessert. What changes about the beam in each of the colors? In which color does the beam travel the farthest? Which color shows the shortest laser beam?

Step 3: Fill the last bowl or a sink with just enough hot water so that when you put the container with the red gelatin into it, the water reaches most of the way up the sides without getting into the container. You don't want the hot water to touch the gelatin. Let the red gelatin container sit for about a minute. Then remove the container from the hot water and place the white plate over the top of it. Carefully invert the container and plate together. Place the plate on your work surface and shake the gelatin container gently until the gelatin releases onto the plate. Be careful, you want the edges of the gelatin to remain smooth.

Step 4: Using the knife, cut the red gelatin circle into two equal semicircles. Set one of the halves aside and keep one on the plate in front of you.

Step 5: Shine the laser into the flat side of the gelatin you just cut. Again, the beam should be parallel to the work surface and the top of the gelatin. Make your observations by looking into the gelatin from above. What happens when the light reaches the curved surface? Slowly move the laser from one end of the cut surface to the other and observe how the trajectory of the light changes with the angle at which it contacts the curved surface.

Step 6: Repeat Step 5, but this time position a piece of white paper behind the curved side of the gelatin. Observe how the beam of light reaching the paper changes as you move the laser across the length of the cut edge of the gelatin.

Step 7: Repeat Steps 5 and 6 several times using the flashlight instead, changing the focus of the beam each time. How does the interaction of the light and the gelatin change when you use white light as opposed to a red light? Your observations should give you an idea of how light moves and how laser beams can travel and reflect. If you were firing a blaster that didn't explode on contact with a surface but reflected depending on the angle, how might this affect your understanding of the weapon and how might you use this information to your advantage?

PLAYING WITH LIGHT

The light and dark sides are different aspects of the Force, but the Force requires the balance of light and dark alike. Did you know that the light we see with our eyes also requires a complex interplay of factors? Light is made up of a variety of colors that become visible to our eyes through different means. When we see red or green we are seeing the color reflected back at us by a specific pigment while other wavelengths are present but absorbed and therefore go undetected by our eyes. And white light is something else altogether. In this activity you'll create your own white light and get an idea of how what we see as the purest of colors really combines many things.

WHAT YOU NEED:

- **Light sticks, one each of red, green, and blue**
- **Small glass bowl**
- **Hammer and nail**
- **Rubber gloves***
- **Goggles***
- **Jar or pencil holder**

TIME REQUIRED: 30 MINUTES

COST:

$ $ $

LEVEL:

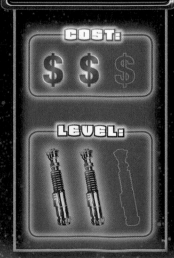

*You're going to be puncturing the light sticks and removing the fluid inside. Wear goggles and gloves at all times when working with the light sticks once they've been punctured.

Step 1: Remove the red, green, and blue light sticks from their wrapping and activate them by bending each one to "snap" open the vial held inside. Shake them to mix the contents of the stick and get a good glow going in each one.

Step 2: Put on your rubber gloves and goggles. Ask an adult to help you puncture the flat end of each light stick by using the hammer and nail. Use the jar or pencil holder to hold the light sticks upright once they've been punctured.

Step 3: Place the small glass dish on your work surface. First, add about ten drops of fluid from the blue light stick by inverting it and shaking the fluid out. Next, add fluid from the green light stick to the bowl a little at a time. Swirl the bowl with each addition to mix the two colors. Observe how the color of the fluid changes as the two colors combine. Stop after you've added about ten

drops. Finally, add fluid from the red light stick a drop at a time and swirl the bowl after adding each drop.

Step 4: Once you've seen how the three mix in this order, try mixing the red and the blue or the red and the green. Wash and dry your bowl before each new combination or use a new bowl for each trial. Try using different amounts of each color and observe the effect on the color of the light that is generated. What do these mixtures tell you about the nature of white light as opposed to light of a specific color?

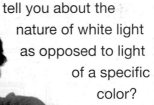

LIFE AFTER FREEZING

Jabba the Hutt keeps Han Solo frozen in carbonite for not repaying a debt. In this frozen state, Han hangs on a wall until his friends rescue him and reverse the freezing process. The Rebel hero suffers from hibernation sickness and is weak at first, but he's otherwise unharmed and able to rejoin the Rebellion. Could a person really be frozen and then brought back to a living state? Try this experiment with plants and see what happens to living tissue when you freeze it.

WHAT YOU NEED:

TIME REQUIRED:
SEVERAL HOURS FOR
FREEZING, 20 MINUTES
FOR OBSERVATIONS

- **Water**

- **Sugar**

- **Small spoon or teaspoon**

- **Freezer**

- **2 clear glass or plastic jars**

- **Masking tape**

- **2 teaspoons of sugar**

- **Several types of plant material such as:**
  - A lettuce leaf
  - A celery stalk
  - Aloe leaf
  - Different leaves from the garden

- **Plastic baggies for each type of plant material**

- **Notebook and pencil**

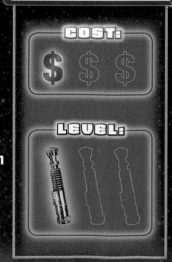

COST:

$ $ $

LEVEL:

120

WHAT TO DO:

Step 1: The first part of this experiment is intended to give you an idea of what happens to water when it freezes. Fill each of your glass or plastic containers about *halfway* with water. Into one jar, add two spoonfuls of sugar and mix until the sugar is dissolved.

Step 2: Use the masking tape to mark the height of the surface of the water in both jars. Place the tape on the jar so the top of the tape lines up with the surface of the water.

Step 3: Put both jars in the freezer and leave for several hours or overnight until they have frozen completely.

Step 4: When the water in both jars has frozen, remove them from the freezer. Observe the surface level of the ice and compare it to where the surface of the water had been. Are the heights the same? If they changed,

did the water and the sugar water change the same amount? What would you say happens to water when it is frozen? What about water that has something dissolved in it?

Step 5: Now you'll see what happens to living cells when they are frozen. Select your different plant parts and place each one in a plastic bag. You can use as few or as many different plants as you like. Observe the characteristics of each and make some notes in your notebook about their qualities before they are frozen. Place the bags in the freezer and leave them for several hours or overnight.

Step 6: Remove the plants from the freezer and let them defrost. You may put them in a warm or sunny spot to speed up the defrosting, or simply leave them on the counter for 30 to 45 minutes. Leaves will not take as long to thaw as thicker plant parts. Once the plants are defrosted, observe the qualities of each one. How do they compare to their qualities before freezing? Record your observations in your notebook. Plants are made up of cells that contain a lot of water with many substances dissolved in it (just like

people!). Knowing what you do about what happens to water when it freezes, how would you explain the change in the plants that takes place after freezing?

If plant cells and animal cells behave similarly when they are frozen, what does that say about our ability to survive a freezing? Would Han Solo have simply suffered from hibernation sickness after being frozen in carbonite, or might there have been even more serious side effects to this treatment?

THE Secret:

Freezing plants causes the water in their cells to expand, which can damage the cell membranes throughout the plant. As a result, the liquid inside the cells seeps out, and the plant, which was given its shape by the rigid structure of the cells, loses its structure and becomes limp. Though there are a few animals out there that can survive being frozen, the list is short and humans are not on it. If you're hoping to keep any prisoners alive, we suggest locking them up rather than freezing them as a way to keep them captive.

BUILD YOUR OWN HOVERCRAFT

On Tatooine, Luke uses a landspeeder to get around. The repulsorlift technology used in this craft allows it to hover just above the ground and travel at high speeds over long distances. We don't have the same technology, but we can tell you how to build a pretty great hovercraft. It won't take you as far or as fast as a landspeeder, but we think it's perfect for something you can build in your own home with easy-to-find materials and equipment.

WHAT YOU NEED:

TIME REQUIRED: 1 HOUR

- Leaf blower
- Inexpensive plywood approximately ½" thick, 3' or 4' square, or precut to a circle 3' or 4' in diameter
- Plastic shower curtain or liner
- Lid to a paint can or large coffee can (more than 30 ounces)
- 4 small nails and a hammer
- Clay or Styrofoam
- Saber saw (preferably electric)
- Pencil
- Electric drill
- Staple gun
- Duct tape
- Foam pipe insulation

COST:
$ $ $

LEVEL:

WARNING: This hovercraft should be built and used with an adult present at all times.

WHAT TO DO:

Step 1: Make the base of your hovercraft out of the plywood. You can keep the base as a square or you can use the saber saw to make a circle.

Step 2: You need to make some holes in the base where you will connect the nozzle of your leaf blower. About halfway between one edge of the base and the center, place the opening of the blower nozzle on the wood and trace it using your pencil. Use the saber saw to cut out this circle.

Step 3: To make the skirt of your hovercraft, lay the shower curtain flat on the floor and place the base on top of it. Fold the edges of the curtain over the base and use the scissors to trim any excess plastic away. You'll want several inches of plastic left to attach to the top of the base.

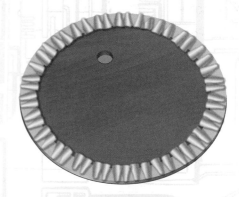

Using the staple gun, secure the plastic around the edge of the top of the base with staples placed every few inches. Once the plastic is secure, use the duct tape to seal the edges so that no air can escape from inside the plastic.

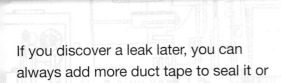

If you discover a leak later, you can always add more duct tape to seal it or to patch any tears in your skirt.

Step 4: Turn the base so the plastic is facing up, and place the paint or coffee can lid in the center. Use the hammer and nails to secure the lid to the base. Use pieces of clay or Styrofoam to cover the points of the nails that stick through to the top side of the base.

Step 6: Use the pipe insulation to create padding around the edge of the base. Simply cut the foam to fit the edges of your craft and use the self-adhesive to hold it in place. This is especially important if you're using a square base, which will have more edges and corners to bump into people and furniture.

Step 5: Cut a circle of 6 openings in the plastic around the lid. These should be evenly spaced in a ring about 3 or 4 inches from the lid.

Step 7: Place the base plastic-side down on the floor and set the nozzle of the blower in the hole you made earlier. Use the duct tape to seal the connection, making sure no air can escape. When you are sitting directly on the plywood, you can hold the blower between your legs or to your side, whichever feels more comfortable and stable.

Step 8: Take flight! Find a large open space with a smooth floor. Linoleum, wood, ceramic tiles, sport courts, or smooth concrete work well. Turn on the leaf blower and feel the base lift into the air. The challenge now is determining how to maneuver the craft to move in the direction you want. Try gently bending the blower nozzle where it attaches to blow the air in different directions and see if you can start directing your movement. Just be careful not to break the seal between the nozzle and the base. Use duct tape for repairs wherever needed.

I think this book is inctrint

INDEX: